THE UNI

CHASING SHADOWS

FROM USA TODAY BESTSELLING AUTHOR
ERIN BEDFORD

Chasing Shadows © 2019 Embrace the
Fantasy Publishing, LLC

Also by Erin Bedford

Curse of the Fairy Tales
Rapunzel Untamed
Rapunzel Unveiled

Her Angels
Heaven's Embrace
Heaven's A Beach
Heaven's Most Wanted

House of Durand
Indebted to the Vampires
Wanted by the Vampires

Academy of Witches
Witching On A Star
As You Witch
Witch You Were Here
Just Witch It

Granting Her Wish
Vampire CEO

THE UNDERGROUND BOOK FOUR

CHASING SHADOWS

FROM USA Today BESTSELLING AUTHOR
ERIN BEDFORD

CHAPTER

KAT

THE TWO MEN standing on my doorstep had to be CIA. Or at least cops. If they were trying to pass as civilians they were failing horribly with their matching black suits and black sunglasses. They each had a crew cut, one brown and one blond, and a stern, no nonsense type of expression on their faces. It didn't make the urge to shut the door lessen.

"What can I help you with?" I repeated. When I had first opened the door I'd been in the middle of a call with my mother and already irritated as fuck by her constant need for me to make more appearances for the Fae community. You'd think that having a Fae for a daughter would make her want me to shy away from the public view, but not Sylvia. It just made her even more determined to make the world see the Fae as normal human beings and not alien invaders like the local news was still spouting out.

Easy to say my greeting of "What?" that was practically shouted didn't set well with the cops. So, I had hung up with my mother and apologized for my rudeness. I still didn't let them in, though. Too many reporters lately had dropped by unannounced wanting to get an interview with the Seelie Princess. I still hadn't found out how that got out, but when I found the person responsible they would be wishing to visit the Bandersnatch.

"Miss Nottington, I am Agent Drake and this is my partner, Agent Walker. We are here on official government business that would be better discussed inside." The blond crew cut said. He put his hands on his hips and there was a slightly uncomfortable grimace on his face. It was the first emotion I had seen on them since I opened the door.

"It's always official business with your type." I gestured a hand up and down at their stuffy suits, not at all feeling underdressed with my sweats and t-shirt that said 'No Talkie Before Coffee.' It was one of my nicer tees, and they were lucky I was wearing clothes at all since it was barely eight a.m.

"Why don't you just make it easier for all of us and just tell me what you want?" I crossed my arms over my chest and waited for them to get to it.

Agent Walker cleared his throat and stepped forward, pulling a piece of paper out of his suit coat. "We have here a letter from the Secretary of Defense, requesting your help in a Fae related matter."

"Fae related matter?" My brow scrunched down as I took the letter from him. It had the official seal of the Secretary, but for all I knew it could be fake. I was an English major and an ex-librarian. Well, hardly an ex-librarian since my career lasted a whole month before I got fired for taking too much time off to deal with Fae drama. When Brandi, my ex-boss and the mean girl of my existence, found out that she had fired the Seelie Princess, she'd had a field day and had wasted no time giving interviews to any reporter that would have her. A tell all about the sadly uneventful life of the human turned fairy princess' life.

At least there wasn't much in my past life as a human to tell all about. I wasn't exactly Miss Popular and preferred to be alone, but Brandi took that and spun it into an intricate tale of high school loner who never quite fit in ends up as the heir to the Seelie kingdom. The press ate it up, and thus, the knocking at my door tripled.

I'd had to get Bar to act as gatekeeper just to keep them off my grandmother's lawn. Since the two men in front of me were on my door step, I made a mental note to check on where the troll was now.

Besides the fact that I was the Fae Princess of the Seelie Court, it didn't exactly make me an expert on official documents. If anything, it would make me less qualified. No matter how much studying I did, my Seelie mother always seemed to be able to pull one over me.

"We can show you our badges if that would help," Agent Walker spouted out, his neutral tone turning to a nervous stutter. So they weren't so nonchalant about being here after all. I forced myself not to grin at the break in their armor.

I frowned at the paper in my hand, the legal jargon not really my area of expertise. I handed it back to them. "You might as well come in. I have no idea what this thing says." I stepped back from the doorway, letting the two into my grandmother's tiny home. I had been living here for about six months now, and she still hadn't returned from her vacation in Florida. She called every once in a while to check in, but every time she seemed happy and seemed to be having the time of her life with no plans to return.

After they came inside, I moved to close the door but not before my eyes swept the front lawn. I frowned. As I thought, Bar was nowhere to be found. The little setup I had put together for him on the front lawn was still there. A blanket with a variety of toys, no chair because Bar was so big he would break anything I could possibly set out for him. The toys were a bribe, one that I was lucky to have figured out the last time he came by when my Seelie mother had ordered him to capture me. To non-friends, Bar was a big ferocious troll that had the

11

mental capacity of a toddler. His three word sentences were pushing it on a good day.

So, I treated him like any child. Gave him candy and toys to sit in my yard and look intimidating. So far, it'd worked pretty well at keeping unwanted guests off my porch. Seeing as the two, possibly FBI agents, were sitting on my couch, it wasn't going well anymore.

Closing the door behind me, I stepped into the living room and surveyed my visitors. Maybe they were secretly Men In Black? At this point, I wouldn't even be surprised if Will Smith showed up at my doorstep asking for my registration to be on this planet. It would actually make my day. I love me some yummy goodness. Not like anything good was going on in my love life these days, not since...

I swallowed down the lump in my throat that had come from letting my thoughts stray to Chess and shoved the pain deep down. Now wasn't the time to get emotional. There were potentially alien cops in my living room that needed to be dealt with. I could cry later over a pint of Ben and Jerry's.

"So..." I started, sitting in the chair across from the two. Agent Walker seemed more nervous by the minute. He had to be new. "...what's all this about?"

"Well, you see," this time Agent Drake stepped in giving his counterpart a warning glance that made him sit back in his seat a bit like a pouting child, "There has been a particularly large outbreak of Fae refugees coming out of the portals all around America, and it has come to the government's attention that there has to be some way to regulate those who are taking up residence in our fair country. We...I mean the Secretary of Defense was hoping as the Seelie Princess and the..."

"Moderator," Agent Walker supplied earning him a glare from his superior.

"As I said, as the Seelie Princess and the Moderator for your kind on this side, they are hoping that you would be forthcoming in helping compile a list of all the Fae residents who have made a home in this world."

"So, you are wanting to know who is Fae and who isn't?" I cocked a brow at them.

"Exactly." Agent Drake nodded his head, seemingly happy that he had explained it right.

"It's not really hard to tell who is Fae and who isn't. I don't know why you need me to help you," I shrugged, "Besides a few half-bloods, most Fae look exactly like they are supposed to. Otherworldly." I gave them a pointed look, telling them how silly I found all this. "A brownie looks like a brownie and a pixie a pixie. Hardly a need for a list when you have your own two eyes to judge what is and isn't Fae."

Agent Walker cleared his throat; his eyes seemed to be asking permission from his partner to speak. Agent Drake gave a short nod indicating that he had permission.

"What my partner is trying to say is that some of the Fae are not so easily distinguished from humans. While, like you said some are easier to spot, others look more or less human, but a more attractive version. Like Miss Erydesa," he paused for a moment as if envisioning her, "with her long, gorgeous fountain of golden hair, and her eyes are so blue that sapphires don't do them justice." His eyes took on a lusty

14

quality that made me cringe. Gab's sure knew how to leave an impression.

Before the, still-didn't-know-if-he-was-a-cop-or-not, could continue on his praise of Gab's endless perfections, his partner elbowed him in the ribs. He winced and rubbed where he had gotten nudged, his face turning red with embarrassment.

"The problem isn't that some of the Fae just look like humans. It's that we aren't able to regulate them as well as we would like," Agent Drake paused for a moment, placing his hands together as he leaned forward in his seat, "What we're asking is for you to make some kind of proclamation telling them to go to a certain place at a certain time so that we may register them as Fae refugees. This will help with policing any Fae who get out of hand and keep our officers safe. They'll know what they're going up against when there's an incident."

I frowned at the agent. I didn't feel right about having to do some kind of proclamation that forced my people to out themselves if they didn't want to be outed by me. It was like saying Irish people had to be registered so the cops would know how to treat them.

I wasn't stupid, I knew exactly what they wanted. Control. They always wanted control over things they didn't understand. But forcing the Fae to register was going too far.

So far they hadn't done anything to provoke the humans. If anything, it was the Fae that should be the ones that were upset. There wasn't a day that I turned on the television that there wasn't a protest or some kind of altercation that ended with a Fae getting hurt. That was usually when the humans were stupid enough to pick on one of the Fae that were bigger than them. I so wasn't about to be part of something like that, government orders or not.

"So say that you get all the Fae registered, what exactly is that going to accomplish? I mean, the Fae that look human could easily use their magic against you before you can even get them close enough to ask for their registration." I crossed my arms over my chest and threw one leg over the other as I leaned back in my chair. "It seems like a waste of time to me."

Agent Drake's face reddened as if he didn't like my answer or that I was questioning what the government had asked. "Now you see here," he shook a finger in my direction, "You Fae came into this world without so much as a lick of thought to any of the humans you were putting in danger, or any of the troubles that you would have caused, or the jobs you're taking by residing in this world. The government has been more than lenient towards your kind, even when you have spread throughout the country and the world without so much as a police force to handle those who get out of hand."

He took a deep breath, the redness of his face deepening with his labored breathing. "You were supposed to go back to where you came from when the danger was over. Instead, you are here, sucking us dry. And if you won't help the problem, you're part of the problem."

He stood to his feet until he was towering over me. I was used to being the smaller person, intimidation tricks like this didn't bother me any. I'd long since gotten over the need to be taller than someone. Being short had it's advantages, like being able to kick someone in the nuts without much effort.

Instead of reacting to his provocation with words, the magic beneath my skin crept up to the top, causing a greenish glow to engulf me. The moment Agent Drake saw my magic, the emotion in his eye confirmed what I'd already assumed based on his words.

While he had tried to put on a front about needing to protect the humans and Fae, he really was afraid. Scared of the unknown, of anyone who dared to be called different. It was his kind, the ones unyielding to change that really pushed my buttons.

I was pleasantly surprised though to see Agent Walker didn't seem afraid at all. In fact, his eyes filled with an excited kind of curiosity. Turning my attention back to the raging brunette officer, I let my magic fill me up. My eyes narrowed. I had no doubt that the blue of my eyes had taken on a fluorescent glow. It caused the officer to fall back in his seat, his scent reeking of terror.

"I will only say this once," I tightened my jaw, "Not now, nor will I ever help you register the Fae. I'm on to your game. First, it is registration, and then you round us up to put us in some kind of concentration camp. The president has assured our safety and residency in this country. And until the time comes that our welcome is no longer valid, then this conversation is completely pointless."

My words did nothing to decrease the fear in the agent's face. If anything, it made his fear turn to anger. He took his stance once more, his rage flowing off him in waves. "Now you see here, girly" he started.

I stopped him by getting to my feet and waving my finger in his face.

"No, it is men like you that kept this country from progressing forward, and I want no part in it. You came to my house asking for my help, and then you insult me and my kind?" I gave a haughty laugh that made the brunette flinch. "You're lucky I don't rip you to shreds right here." I clucked my tongue at him, the urge to use my magic becoming overwhelming.

"Is that a threat?" he roared.

"You bet your sorry ass it is," I shot back. "Now get the hell out of my grandmother's house."

The younger agent scrambled to his feet and tried to steer the other agent towards the door. The stubborn ass jerked his arm away, and snarled, "No, I'll leave when I'm good and ready. And that will be when you agree to this order."

"Oh?" I drew out, "it's an order now, is it?" I cocked my head to the side; his words were the last straw in a long list of insults.

"Yes, and as a US citizen you are expected to obey." A mean smile curled up on his face, and it made me only too happy to react.

The magic that had barely been contained in my skin flew out and wrapped around Agent Drake's body. He struggled against it, trying to get some kind of grip, but as his hand went through it, he cursed and screamed at me. The other officer was smart enough to scramble for the door, not waiting to be personally escorted out. Not leaving my spot in the living room, I hurled the officer across the room, out the open door, and slammed it firmly shut behind him.

Releasing my built up magic, I collapsed into my chair with an aggravated sigh. I didn't know why I was surprised. I knew it was bound to happen eventually. I just didn't think it'd be this soon. We were going to have to come to some kind of agreement or all hell was going to break loose. The leash I had on my Fae mother was short at best, and there was only so much that I could do on my own. This was one of those times I really wished Chess were here; he'd know what to do.

CHAPTER

CHESS

I SCREAMED AT Kat's reflection in the mirror while pounding my fists against the glass. She was washing her hands in the bathroom, and she didn't even look up at me. With an aggravated cry I slammed my hands down hard against the glass, but it didn't move or crack. It was as if I'd barely hit it at all.

"I don't know why you even bother?" Morgana commented behind me.

My scowl deepened as I stared at the barren floor of the Shadow Realm. Not looking up I said, "What else am I going to do?"

"I don't know, but I have a few ideas." She pressed her body against the side of mine, her ample breasts shoved into my arm that was holding onto the side of the mirror.

Morgana had stopped trying to be subtle the last few months. Compared to the time in Kat's world it felt more like years, and Morgana had spent every waking moment trying to get into my pants. A lesser Fae would have been tempted, and if I was anything, I was a lesser Fae. If she'd caught me a year ago before I had met Kat I would have taken her up on her offer.

Now, that I've known love and melded my magic with Kat's, the thought of touching anyone else disgusts me. Not to forget the gaping hole in my heart that seemed to widen every day we were apart.

"I've told you once and I'll tell you again. Not now or will I ever be with you." I shoved off the glass with my tail wagging in aggravation behind me. I marched out of the mirror graveyard.

I didn't look to see if she would follow. She was the only person that I'd seen since my arrival, and as far as I knew, I was the only company she had. I knew she'd come after me eventually.

The days in the Shadow Realm were always the same. I'd wake up disoriented and for a moment forget where I was. When I remembered the ache in my chest knocks me breathless, and I had to fight to drag in each agonizing breath. Eventually, I am able to move without pain and crawl out of bed.

I pretend to eat the slop that Morgana gives me each morning. The Reaper only knows where she gets the ingredients for it, and then I spend the rest of my day trying to get through one of the mirrors. Every hour just trying to get somebody to see that I'm trapped, that I'm still here. I'm not dead. At least, Morgana says I'm not anyways. It's the one thing I actually believe that comes out of her mouth. The rest was too obscure to even consider. At the end of the day, I would lay down for a night of restless sleep filled with nightmares, only to wake up to do it all over again.

"You should be nicer to me." Morgana slithered up beside me. I didn't have to look to know that the crimson dress she wore almost everyday clung to her like a second skin. It pushed up her breasts until they threatened to come clean out of the top. It was one of her tricks to try and get me to accept her advances. Too bad for her I was more into the subtle sex appeal. Like Kat.

"And why is that?" I asked glancing sideways at her.

She flicked her long black hair over her shoulder with a coy smile. "Because eventually you will get tired of trying to get out, and then you'll want me, and I might not want you then."

I scoffed. "I'll never get tired of trying. I will always try to get out and get back to her." I made my words firm and unyielding, trying to make her believe them as much as myself.

"You say that now, but believe me, it won't last. Do you think I became Queen of the Shadow Realm overnight?" She waved her hands over her form in an exaggerated manner. "I had a family that was waiting for me on the other side too. And no matter how much I tried, no matter how much I screamed and begged, they never knew I was here. They just went on with their lives as if I never existed."

The bitterness in her voice surprised me. She had always acted like she didn't have a care in the world. Well, besides getting me to sleep with her. The whole Queen of the Shadow Realm thing was a joke. Even if it was true, there was no one else here but me and her. The Reaper only knew where the prince had ended up if he was here at all.

"So tell me, Morgana," I tried to not let the disdain I felt for her come through, "What is it that you are here?"

I'd asked her the question before, several times in fact, but she would always give me an evasive answer. Sometimes it was about how she was born here. Another time she had said she had just found her way here or some other nonsense like that. This was the first time that she had made any mention having a prior life or family back in the Underground.

She stepped in front of my path blocking me from going further. Her hand slid up my chest and tangled in my pale hair. I stood as stiff as a board but didn't push her away as I waited to see if she would answer.

"Just say I rejected the wrong person," she murmured as she pushed up on her tiptoes and tried to press her lips to mine. I turned my face and she kissed the side of my cheek.

"And who would that be?"

"Give me a kiss and I'll tell you." She smirked at me.

"I don't want to know that badly. In fact, I don't really want to know at all." I reached out to remove her arms from around me, but she dropped her arms from around my neck first with a huff.

Morgana pursed her lips then let out a sigh. "Fine. You're no fun."

"Have I ever been?" Inwardly, I was laughing at myself. Cheshire S. Cat wasn't fun? The audacity of it was unimaginable. The fact was that being here had caused me to become a party pooper, rightly killing my former self. I missed it but it was necessary. There were more important things than having fun. Like getting back to Kat.

"If you're going to tell me, no more games."

Her eyes went to my chest where she walked her fingers across the muscles as she said, "You know the Reaper's a nice guy once you get to know him, quite handsome too. Though, he has a nasty temper."

The Reaper? What did he have to do with any of this? Then before I could ask her, I stopped and realized what she had just said. I looked down at her, my eyes widening. "You rejected the Reaper?"

"Everyone makes mistakes." Morgana shrugged one shoulder and turned away from me and walked back towards the place she called home.

It wasn't much more than a hovel. A door shoved into a dirt mound but with nothing else around but the graveyard of mirrors, it was precariously out of place. Where she got any of the stuff to create her home was just as much a mystery as what she fed me every day. For all I knew, she materialized it out of nowhere. Maybe the Reaper was her parts supplier. He was probably the only one who knew why my magic didn't work down here.

I had tried to de-materialize Between Worlds so many times my head ached. I couldn't even get halfway there. When I tried to use it I didn't even feel the familiar pull at my energy. Either something was stopping my magic, or it simply just wasn't there anymore. Morgana hadn't been very forthcoming with information on that front either.

"If you know the Reaper then where is he?" I waved a hand around us as if he should be in the very place we stood. "Where does he dwell?"

I followed her as she walked into the hovel and then she splayed herself out across the bed and crooked her fingers towards me. "Come lay next to me, and I'll tell you all about it."

The hovel only had one bed. When I had first arrived I had spent painful nights on the floor refusing to share a bed with her, but then after several days of waking up with aches and pains, I relented. At first, she tried her best to come on to me, accidentally brushing my body with her own, pretending she didn't know I was there. Thankfully, when it was clear that I wasn't going to accept her advances, she kept her hands to herself, at least during the night. During the day was a whole different story.

I didn't want to give her any false hopes that I was finally coming around when all I wanted was information. I didn't want to be stuck here forever. If she was withholding

29

information that could help me get out, I was going to get it one way or the other. I was Cheshire S. Cat. When the queen was forcing her Seelie on me I had been the best pretender in all the Underground. I was good at making others think I was interested when really I was just waiting for it to be over so I could get what I wanted. I'd played the game for years; I could do it for a few more minutes. At least to get what I needed, and then I was out of here.

I sat down on the edge of the bed and glanced back at her with a wary stare. "All right, I'm on the bed tell me."

"No, no," Morgana patted the bed next to her, "Lay down, take a load off from screaming and banging at the mirror, you can take a rest for just one day, can't you?

I let out a frustrated growl as I swung my legs up over the side of the bed and lay next to her, trying to keep as much distance between us as possible. The moment I did, she moved over until the full length of her body was pressed up against my side, making sure I felt every curvature of her form.

"Now isn't that better," she purred, trailing her hand up and down my chest.

My ears twitched as I forced myself not to roll my eyes. "If you say so. Now will you tell me?"

As she settled in against me, as if she were planning to stay a while, she hummed, "I don't know. What were we talking about again?"

"You were telling me where the Reaper lives, but I'm starting to think you don't even know." I moved to get up but her hands were quick to keep me on the bed.

"Don't be so hasty. You know you really should learn to lighten up. When you're stuck down here for eternity, you have to at least try to find some enjoyment in it. Spending every day trying to reach the other side is going to drive you mad."

I gave her a stony glare. In return, she huffed and laid her head against my shoulder. Her hair fanned out around her as she looked up at me from beneath her lashes. "The Reaper really isn't somebody you want to mess with, even if it's to get home. He doesn't take kindly to strangers, especially not Fae."

The fact that the Reaper didn't like strangers was laughable. Wasn't it his job to take souls to the other world? How did he handle his daily job if he couldn't stand people? An introvert forced to interact with others, there was nothing more ironic.

I said to her, "I'll take my chances. How do I get to him?"

"You don't really think I'm going to tell you, do you? As soon as I do, you'll go running off on your own and get yourself killed. You won't last five minutes in this graveyard." She gave a haughty laugh.

"What do you know?" I pushed away from her and off the bed. "You just sit here day after day doing nothing. Did you even try to get out? To get home? Or are you so full of yourself that nobody would want you even if you came back?"

Morgana's eyes narrowed on me as she leaned on her elbows. "You don't know what you're talking about. You don't know who I am or anything about me. And I won't be responsible for your rash decisions."

"Then why bring it up at all," I growled clenching my teeth together, my tail whipping behind me in rapid movements as I tried to restrain my anger.

"Because I'm tired of seeing you pout and scream. You're not the only one here, you know. I've had to listen to your nightmares every night. I haven't slept a decent night's sleep in months," she moved her hands over her face, her fingers touching the skin beneath her eyes, "I'm starting to get bags. Next thing you know, I'll be all wrinkly. No one's going to even want me and then where will I be?"

"Why won't you help me then?" I snarled, not caring for her whining.

"I didn't say I wasn't going to help you, I just said I wasn't going to tell you where he was. That doesn't mean that I won't show you." She smoothed her hands down her dress to get the non-existent wrinkles out of it, and then Morgana circled around the bed to the other side of the room.

She opened the door to her closet and started digging around. I stood there with my arms crossed, tapping my foot and patiently waiting until she finally pulled out what she was looking for. She held up some clothing that I had never seen before and then started to disrobe.

I turned my back on her quickly, remembering her game. More than once she had caught me off guard by taking her clothes off at random. Supposedly, she would be itchy or have spilled something on them. I didn't believe it for a second. Where she even got all her clothes from was another wonder of the Shadow Realm. It made me long for my own expansive wardrobe.

"I'm done, you can turn around now." At her bitter words, I slowly turned around with my hands up over my face to make sure she was actually dressed. I was surprised by how conservative her clothing was. From the moment I arrived here she'd worn plunging necklines and dresses with high slits, but what she was wearing now wouldn't even make a school kid blush.

Wearing brown slacks and low heeled shoes, her forest green long sleeve shirt only had a slight scoop. It hardly showed any cleavage whatsoever. She took her long black hair and pulled it up into a high ponytail so that the ends of it skimmed the back of her neck.

"If I'd known you were going to stare, I would have changed into clothing like this before," she teased me with a wink.

My lips dipped into a frown as I turned away from her and toward the door.

"Just come on," I commanded before stopping at the door. When she came up behind me, I swung the door open with a mocking bow. "After you, your highness."

CHAPTER

3

KAT

GOING TO CHESS' grave was always hard. Not that visiting a deceased loved one was easy for anyone, but I found it particularly hard since we never got to bury his body.

I used to go every day, now I was lucky to get there once a week. It made me feel guilty for my lack of attendance. The other Fae brought him new flowers and gifts for the vine encased throne. It still sat under the willow tree that was created in his memory. I'd never had to make sure it was cleaned off, because someone was keeping it pristine.

It made me happy to know others cared so much about him but also mad, because it should be my job. I should be the one making sure his grave was cared for. The one who should be by every day just to talk to him. But even I knew that my heart couldn't take it. The times I did come out were hard enough.

Sometimes I would come out here just to talk to him about nothing at all. Whether or not he could actually hear me I didn't know. I would tell him about my day or some crazy thing my mother had done. Sometimes I'd come out here to vent about the things I just couldn't handle. But most the time I came out here when I missed him.

It was usually near the end of the day, when I should be going to bed, but instead I would curl up in a ball on the throne as if just being there made me close to him. I would cry until my throat was raw and my eyes burned. This was one of those times.

I'd been here for at least a couple hours and my sobs had slowly ceased. I stayed here in his throne, my insides calm except for the gaping hole in my chest where he should be.

"I told you it was going to be like this," a deep, sultry voice caused my head to jerk up from the throne, Mab, the UnSeelie Queen, stood before me. Still looking very much the queen in her black on black pantsuit, she scanned the area with her sapphire eyes. They were the same exact shade as her son's. I suddenly remembered that I wasn't the only one who had lost somebody. She'd lost her son.

"What are you doing here?" I asked wiping my face with the back of my hand as I sat up.

"Why visiting the human world. I thought it was all the rage this year." Her lips twisted into a grim smile, sarcasm dripping from her words.

"Yeah, but I didn't think that you would come. My mother sure hasn't."

"That's the difference between your mother and I. What kind of queen would I be if most of my citizens were over here and I was in the Underground?" She tutted and shook her head. "I can't very well keep my eye on them in another world."

Mab wasn't like my mother, Tatiana, the Seelie Queen. She couldn't give a rat's ass about the Fae in the human world as long as they weren't causing trouble in the Underground. Besides, she was too busy trying to find ways around the newly formed Council that was blocking her every move in regards to the Kingdom.

In that way Mab was the better Queen, the better ruler. She didn't overstep her bounds, and she cared more for her people's safety than her own. If the government knew that she was here now they would be scrambling over themselves to capture her. She would be great leverage in getting their little registration thing going.

The fact that they hadn't tried to capture me showed that at least they had some brains in their head when it came to the Fae. They wanted me on their side and knew that taking me would cause uproar. It was pretty ridiculous in my opinion, even though Chess had been the one that had given his life to save them, I was still the one they revered and sometimes to my chagrin, feared.

I suppose it was better for them to fear me than hate me. I hadn't done much in the aspect of things to cause any hatred. I hadn't done much of anything since I'd left.

I had pretty much practiced my magic and tried to avoid my mothers'. The human one kept trying to get me more involved with the Fae community while the other one kept trying to call me through the mirror. I had them covered unless I needed them. Last time I had a mirror call from her it hadn't ended so well for either of us.

"But like I was saying," Mab continued as she walked across the green grass in front of the throne before kneeling down to where the other Fae had laid gifts and flowers, "I told you what you were in for before you gave your magic to that feline. It won't get any better." She glanced up at me seriousness on her face before she focused her attention back to the ground. She placed her hand on the ground. A glittery blue energy spread out from it and into the ground, and when she lifted her hand a single white rose lay its place.

"I don't expect it to," I replied to her, my awe of her skill masterfully masked.

"If you say so," she shrugged and then stood from the ground and dusted off her knees, "Now, how are you going to get our boys back?"

My eyebrows scrunched together as I stared at her. "What do you mean get them back? They're dead. There is no getting them back."

"Dead and *dead* are two different things. You sent them back to where they came from, right?"

"Yeah, that's what the spell was supposed to do. Send the Shadows back to where they belong."

"And where exactly do the Shadows belong?" Mab crossed her arms over her chest and waited like a patient teacher. I really wished people would stop asking questions they already knew the answers to. It would be so much easier if they would just tell me what they knew right away instead of making me run around like a chicken with its head cut off trying to figure out on my own.

"Shadows go to the Shadow Realm, and that means they're not dead. They're just..." she fluttered her hand in the air, "...misplaced."

I stared in disbelief, "Misplaced? Is that what you call it?"

When I had done the spell given to me by my Seelie mother I'd expected myself to go

41

with the Shadows if I didn't have the strength to keep my feet planted firmly on the ground. It was the Shadow man who had the last laugh, though. Chess' blood had been on my hands when I had cast the spell, making it so that he was the sacrifice instead of myself. The spell had done its job. It got rid of the Shadow man and took Chess with him, leaving me in a devastated state.

I was still trying to get used to the idea that Chess and Dorian were both gone. Dorian and I hadn't exactly seen eye-to-eye at the end, and I had pretty much broken his heart, but I didn't mean I wanted him stuck in the Shadow Realm forever. It wasn't something I would wish on anybody, except the Shadow man since I had sent him there. If Mab thought that I was going to scramble all over myself because she gave me some kind of cryptic message about them not being dead she had another thing coming.

"It's been over six months and we haven't heard anything from either of them. They aren't coming back." I shook my head and stood from the throne.

"So, you are just going to give up like that? I thought you loved the cat, and at one point you loved my son as well."

"Yeah, I mean, I did," I stumbled over my words, trying to make her understand, "But that doesn't make them alive. Just all the more reason why I shouldn't be barking up the wrong tree and getting hope where there's not any. I have enough on my plate with both my mothers' hounding me, and now the government is banging down my door trying to get me to help them with Fae registration."

"Fae registration?" Mab's lips twisted at the words.

"Yes, some bullshit about wanting to keep track of us so they can regulate the Fae better," I paused, throwing my hands up in the air, "It's a bunch of political bullshit and a tiny piece of paper."

"Yes, I can see how that would be a problem. We don't even have anything like that in the Underground. Most of us can tell what the other person is without having to ask, let alone needing to write it down." She tapped her face with her long blood red nail. "But the fact that they want to register us doesn't bode well. This should be brought up with the council," she turned to leave but then stopped and looked back at me, "I'm going to go talk to the council about this. Don't forget about what I said. You can get them back, I know you can, you just have to believe it."

Oh yeah, I believed it. Me and Peter Pan.

AFTER MY LOVELY conversation with Mab, I hurried back home to find Alice and Hatter snuggling on the couch. The moment they saw me they jumped apart as if struck by lightning. Alice's face turned beet-red and she stared at the floor. Hatter, on the other hand, had a pensive expression on his face like he hadn't been caught red-handed.

"Don't mind me," I said smirking at them as I made my way across the living room to grab a bottled water from the fridge. "I'm just going to go take a shower."

Alice called out to me before I could get out of the living room, "Did the queen find you?"

"You knew she was coming?" I placed my hands on my hips and glared at her. "And you didn't think it was a good idea to warn me?"

She shrugged a shoulder and shot back, "It's not like it was your mother."

"Yeah, well, a bit of a heads-up would have been nice. It wasn't exactly a conversation I wanted to have at Chess' grave." I took a drink from my water bottle and then wiped my mouth. "I'm actually glad that the two of you are here. Seeing Mab reminded me that there is still a big gaping hole in the middle of the UnSeelie Court, which can't be good for anyone."

"I would imagine not," Hatter spoke up, "You never know who might wander through and into the Between. The longer it is open the likelihood of you having to go after them rises."

Sadly, he was right. As the certified savior of the Underground, if someone ended up in the Between because of the mess I left behind when fighting the Shadow man, whether or not I made the mess didn't matter, I was going to have to go after them.

"Hence my problem," I pointed at him. "Do either of you know anything about how to go about closing that hole at Chess' Willow Tree?"

45

Hatter tapped a finger on his chin; his silver eyes flickered, making them look like liquid steel. When he spoke each word was enunciated perfectly and with precision, "Not that I am aware of. The ability to rip a hole between the worlds is not commonly done. In fact, only a few Fae have ever been able to do such a thing."

"Oh, oh." Alice jumped up and down in her seat. She lifted her arm and waved her hand at me. "I bet you Pat is one of those. Don't you think? He makes the mirrors that go between the worlds and that's kind of like a hole, right?"

I cocked my head to the side as I thought about her suggestion. The short grumpy man I had met in Summerville did indeed have the power to create portals out of mirrors. I wasn't sure if that equated to ripping a hole in the fabric of space itself, if that's what you could call what the Shadow man had done. Not that I had anything against Pat but going to the Seelie Court was not on my list of things to do anytime soon.

"I guess we could ask him. I mean, if anything maybe he knows somebody who could help us. Maybe there is some kind of magical Band-Aid I can use to close the portal back up. Not that it's really bothering anyone being there at the moment."

Hatter spoke up at my words, his voice ominous and dark, "The door to the Between is not simply there to monitor our goings and comings. There are things that should stay between."

That was helpful. I'd only been in the Between a few times, and it hadn't been pleasant. The only thing I really knew about it was if you went too far away from where the doors stood you might never come back again. I'd almost gone out there once.

The first time that I entered the Between there had been some kind of Dark Shadow that I had tried to go after, but the receptionist, the two-headed bird sisters, had warned me away. Those two still hadn't shown back up yet, nor had any of the others that had been taken by the Shadow man. We all just assumed that they had gone to the Shadow Realm as well. A lot more people had perished then I would like to admit in my game with the shadows. I couldn't let it happen again. Having the portal closed would keep us that much safer, so I'd better find a way to close it and fast.

"All right then," I clapped my hands together having come to a decision, "My shower can wait. I'm going to try and see if I can get a hold of Pat and then go from there. You guys just continue doing whatever it was you were doing before I came into the room," I waggled my eyebrows suggestively at them causing Alice to blush as she peeked over at Hatter's form.

The romance between the two seemed to have blossomed overnight. I had always suspected Alice had a thing for Hatter. The last time we visited him at his house they had been holding hands but any other kind of PDA had been kept to a minimum and behind closed doors. I was just waiting for the day that I caught them making out on my couch, so I would finally be able to tease Alice with something, instead of her always getting on my case about my silly human ways.

The door closed behind me as I entered my bedroom. I glanced over to the mirror that I had replaced when my mother had stolen Chess. Thinking about him and how he'd been tortured in the Bandersnatch, caused a stinging pain in my heart.

I promised to never let anything else happen to him again because of me, but apparently, my promises didn't mean anything. He still got hurt because of me, and now he was lost because of me, and there was nothing I could do about it.

I pulled the sheet off the mirror slowly, half expecting my mother to pop up at any moment. She had been trying for days now to contact me. No doubt for some silly and nonsensical rule she wanted to pass but the council wouldn't let her. Apparently, I had veto power when it came to the council. But if there was something that my mother wanted to be done, and they didn't approve of it, I was pretty sure that I wasn't going to agree either.

I heaved a big sigh when nothing jumped out at me right away, and I moved my hand up the side of the mirror. I pushed my magic into the frame, activating it. The glass rippled and danced for a moment before the reflection of my bedroom changed into a window into Pat's shop.

Mirrors, frames, and other gadgets filled the shelves and floor of the shop. From my own personal experience, I knew that beyond the edges of the mirror it was even more cluttered, and I still had the bruises to prove it.

"Pat," I called out, but no one showed up in front of the mirror. "Are you home?"

There was some banging and pounding off to the side before there was a smash. It was followed by a string of curses. The voice could only belong to one person. Pat.

"I'm coming. Hold on," he shouted from somewhere off to the side of the mirror's edge.

I sat on the bed waiting patiently for him to finish whatever it was that I had interrupted him doing. I didn't have to wait long before his face showed up in the mirror.

"Yeah, what do you want?" He griped as soon as he saw my face. The goggles wrapped around his face pulled his gray hair back. Dirt smudges were smeared across his cheeks and nose from whatever he had been working on. A utility belt with different tools hung around his waist, some of which I had never seen before and some as common as a hammer. The one time I had interacted with Pat had been brief and unpleasant. He had only helped me before because of my father; I could only hope he would still continue to do so now.

"Hey, Pat. Sorry to interrupt you," I started before he cut me off.

"No, you're not. Just tell me what you want. I'm busy."

I didn't like the snarky attitude he was directing toward me when I was trying to be pleasant, which was a huge achievement on my part. So I dropped the nice girl face.

"It might have come to your attention that there's a big ass hole in the middle of the UnSeelie Court about where the moderator lived. Do you know anything about it?"

Pat fiddled with something in his hand, not looking at me as he snapped, "Yeah, what about it?"

"Well, it needs to be closed up before someone gets any smart ideas about going in it. Got any ideas how to do that?"

He looked at me for a moment before he scoffed, "Oh, I get it. Pat here can make mirror portals; he must know all things about portals. Let's go to Pat and bug him, because he has nothing better to do."

"Well, yeah." I shrugged being blunt about it.

"Well, you could try reading a book sometime," he snorted waving the screwdriver he had in his hand at me, "You spent enough time in your library when you were younger, you'd think you would know how to read a book."

"What are you talking about?" I shook my head at him. "There are no books in the Seelie Library about how to close up holes." I would know, as he said I spent most of my childhood, and the majority of my adult Fae life in the library. If there was a book in there about closing holes between worlds then I would know about it.

Pat snorted at my response, clearly becoming impatient. "You weren't looking in the right places. Go to the library and look for a book by Phineas Portalus. You'll find what you need." He pulled his goggles back down over his face with a frown. "Now if you don't mind. I have orders that need to be filled and no more time for you."

Before I could ask another question the mirror went black and my confused face reflected back at me. Well, that was helpful. Who the heck was Phineas Portalus?

CHAPTER

CHESS

THE SHADOW REALM was more than just Morgana's hovel and the graveyard of mirrors. The surrounding areas were dark and full of a dense fog that made it impossible to see where you were walking.

When I first arrived in the Shadow Realm I had woken up in the mirror graveyard with no idea where I was. The ground was cold and covered with dirt. My body had ached from where the Jabberwocky's claws had torn up my side. That's where Morgana found me.

She had taken me to her home and patched me up. I should be grateful to her, but she had made it clear the first day that she was selfish and only had her own interests at heart. She'd only saved me so she wouldn't die of boredom.

The first two days were kind of a blur and filled with a range of emotions. Angry that the Shadow Man had once again tricked us, and then there was the sorrow that had grown stronger every day. It only got worse when I found out about the mirrors.

Wallowing in self-pity, I would spend hours in front of them, hoping for a chance to see Kat. To get her to hear me, but like Morgana had pointed out, she never did.

One day I had wandered away from the mirrors to the edge of the graveyard. There was nothing out there but dense fog, no movement or light. Tired of waiting for the mirrors to get my message through, I had decided it had to be better out there than being stuck in here. I placed a foot into the fog and the moment that I touched it, a chill ran up my spine. The hairs on my arms stood up and a deep, unsettling, nauseating fear pulled at my gut.

I had tried to push the feeling away but it gnawed at me, and then the final straw was a growl off in the distance that had me pulling my foot back to the graveyard. Whether it was magic forcing me to stay here or my own cowardice I didn't know, but I hadn't tried to leave ever since.

Now, Morgana led me out of her house and straight to the edge of the fog. I slowed my pace behind her when I saw where she was going, apprehension gripping at my throat. Morgana didn't seem to have the same hang-ups as I did. She stepped right up to the edge without a care in the world. Unlike with me, if she felt anything when she stepped in she didn't show it, and once she was fully covered something peculiar happened. The air around her cleared leaving a small area around her clear.

"Are you coming or what?" she called over her shoulder as she stepped further into the darkness.

I hesitated, not wanting to have that sickening feeling again, but then I stuck my foot out into the area that was still clear. When I didn't feel it, I let out the breath I hadn't known I was holding and quickly followed after her.

"Why is it that you can go through the fog?" I asked following close behind her, my eyes darting to the darkness around us. "Doesn't it make you feel..."

"Sick?" she supplied and then shook her head, her ponytail wagging behind her.

"Yes." I ignored the urge to bat the bobbing hair away and asked, "Why aren't you affected by it?"

"Because I belong here and you don't," she stated not supplying me with any more details causing irritation to build in me.

"If I don't belong here then why am I here? Shouldn't there be some kind of person to make sure that kind of thing doesn't happen?" My boots crunched on the ground beneath my feet, the dirt having turned into dried grass. It was sad to admit that the sight of grass, even dead grass, made my heart swell with joy.

"You mean a moderator?" she said with a hint of laughter in her voice. The way she said it made me think that she knew exactly who I was and had been playing with me this whole time.

"Yes, like a moderator." My teeth ground together as I said the words. I could have lashed out at her and asked her what I suspected she knew, but I was trying to get information out of her. Being a cad was not going to win me any points.

"Hmm, well I suppose you can say we have one, but they don't come by often, and it's pretty much up to us to moderate ourselves. Besides, it's not like we have unexpected visitors, like yourself, often."

I grabbed her arm, forcing her to stop and turn to me. "So why then, if you are supposed to be in charge of your own stuff, haven't you helped me get out of here before? Did you just keep me here for your own amusement? Is this some sort of game to you?" My previous decision to charm her was thrown out the window as my emotions overcame my need for answers.

She didn't respond the way that I would have thought. She didn't jerk her arm away from me and claim her status as Queen of the Shadow Realm and she could do what she liked. No, what she did was far worse.

Her lips curled up into a nasty smile, and her eyes glinted with mischief. "All of life's a game. Only some of us are lucky enough to know who's playing. Wouldn't you like to play with me, my little kitty cat?"

The words she spouted back at me were almost the exact words I had said to Kat when we had first met in the UnSeelie Court. How did she know what I said? Instead of asking her, I dropped her arm and snarled, "Not with you. Never with you."

Shrugging, she turned back toward the invisible path she was leading me down as if our conversation had never happened. "Anyways, you feel fear because that is the way the magic works here. It is supposed to keep those who don't belong out."

"So, then where are we going?" Irritation still prickled my voice, but at least she was answering most of my questions. If I lashed out again I had no doubt she wouldn't have a problem leaving me here.

"You wanted to go to the Reaper, so I am taking you to the Reaper's. It just so happens the way is through this mess." She fluttered her hand at the fog around us. Surprisingly, it hadn't closed in on me as I thought it would, since as she said, I 'didn't belong', but instead kept the area open. Just in case, I tried to keep a close distance between us but not so close she'd get any ideas.

I let her lead me through the fog for a while, our conversation having died off with her last explanation. I figured I'd find out what was going on when we got there and no sooner. Not that it wasn't eating me up to ask her. Curiosity killed the cat as they say, and this cat wasn't going to be doing any dying anytime soon. Once was enough.

Eventually, the fog cleared to a large area about the size of Morgana's place. Also, like hers, there was a mirror graveyard and a hovel like home. Seeing this caused me to wonder if that was the standard for living in the Shadow Realm. Crappy living quarters and mirrors that tortured you with your friends and family being so close but so far away. If there was a hell, I had no doubt I had found it.

"Hello, boys," Morgana called out with a bit of a singsong voice. Her hips moved in exaggerated movements that reminded me of a slithering snake.

My steps behind her slowed as I watched the door to the hovel open to reveal two men. Exactly identical they had dark brown hair and piercing green eyes. They had well-defined jaws and enough muscles to crush me like a bug. I instantly didn't like them, or the way they looked at me like I was something they found at the bottom of their shoe.

When they saw Morgana their eyes lit up, and their lips curled into feral grins. Their eyes scanned up and down her form as if they were in the desert and she was the first glass of water they had seen in years. Just the sight of it made me cringe. Apparently, Morgana frequented these fellows often. What they did together I didn't want to know.

"Morgana," one of the men said as he came up to her side and wrapped an arm around her waist. The possessive hold he had on her made me think he thought I was competition. I wanted to speak up that he could gladly have her but knew he wouldn't believe me so I kept my mouth shut.

"Who is your...friend." His gaze shot to me, accusation in his look. When she threw her head back and laughed, his eyes turned back to the woman in his arms.

"He is hardly a friend, more like an unwelcome prisoner." She placed her hand on his chest, her eyes sliding over to me giving me a silent warning that I didn't understand. She let herself be embraced by the man before the other one came up beside her wanting the same welcome. She gladly switched between their arms, not seeming to care how their hands roamed on her form.

"We could take him off your hands if you like," the other one growled, the threat clear in his voice as he glared at me.

"No, no. I have to take him to the Reaper. He will want to know we have trespassers in any case." She patted his massive chest and then moved out of his arms. "Cheshire, this is Carban and Coby," she gestured to each one in turn and then grasped each of their hands with a happy smile, "They are my special friends."

Special wasn't all that they were, I was sure, but I didn't comment and just nodded my head, a playful grin disguising my true thoughts. "Pleasure."

"Cheshire," she continued explaining to the men who were completely enamored by her, "is trying to get home to his lady love. He's been trying for months, you should have seen him, the poor dear." The pity in her voice made me want to call her out on her lies as she pouted at me. If she had been sad for me any of the time I was stuck at her place she sure had a sorry way of showing it. All she did was taunt me and try to seduce me. Not once had she shown an ounce of sympathy for my plight.

One good thing that came from her mockery was the twins' faces changed from competitive to empathetic. They nodded their heads as she told my story, the emotion on their face showing they knew exactly how I felt.

"We feel your pain friend," the one named Carban said, "I am lucky to have been exiled with my brother, Coby. Others like our Morgana here are not so lucky and are stuck alone forever to be haunted by their past lives. I do not know what I would have done had I not had my brother to help me through the lonely times." He clamped a hand on his brother's shoulder with a grateful grin, which his brother returned.

"Yes, we are truly blessed," Coby agreed before turning to Morgana. "Will you dine with us before you head out? Or are you in much of a hurry?"

"Oh, I don't know. We have a ways to go, and I don't want to be out here too long. You know what can happen," Morgana said ominously before she glanced over at me with a sly grin, one that I knew meant we were staying whether I liked it or not. "But I guess we could stay a little while, that is if it's okay with Cheshire?"

I didn't dare say no. I might not be the smartest Fae in the Underground, but I wasn't stupid. If I was the one who said no then the twins would have reason to dislike me, and I needed all the friends I could get if I planned to get home and back to Kat.

So instead of shouting what I wanted to say, I gave them a fanged tooth grin and said, "I would be delighted."

CHAPTER

5

KAT

ALICE OFFERED TO come with me to the library, but I declined. For the first time ever I'd be going into the Underground by myself. No Trip or Mop to stand by my side as I ventured through the unknown terrain. No Seer to command the guards to let me pass or to lead me by the hand.

It was frightening and exhilarating at the same time. Like the feeling you get when you are jumping from a high place without a net. You hope you'll be fine. You think you'll be fine, but at the same time, there is a sense of fear that you will be squashed into a pancake on the floor.

Fortunately, I didn't have to go through the Between to get to the Seelie Court. One thing I had been able to convince Pat to do was to make my mirror versatile. He had made it so I could go to any active mirror in the Underground or human world. Which apparently, he told me there were more and more requests for it every day. It was something that I probably should look into later, being the moderator and all. It probably wasn't a good idea to have Fae jumping back and forth across the United States causing mayhem wherever they went. I already had the government on my back; I didn't need any more trouble.

Pat assured me that the mirror would take me straight to the library, and I wouldn't have to go through any of the hallways that might possibly make me run into my mother. I had no fantasies about the fact that I probably wasn't getting in and out of the Library without seeing my mother. I measured the likelihood of not seeing her somewhere between not likely and no way in hell. All I could do was step into the mirror and hope that whatever I encountered I would come out in one piece.

Taking a deep breath I slid my hand across the edge of the frame while thinking about the library that I'd gone to with Alice. It was a large room but smaller than the ballroom. The two floors of it were covered with wall-to-wall bookshelves, full of so many books that it was more than I could count or imagine.

As a child, I used to spend almost all of my time there. Lost in the adventures of the pages before me, I dreamed of the day that I would get to leave the Seelie Palace. It used to be my safe place, for me and my father. Now, all it did was remind me of the girl I once was and the woman I am now.

I held onto that thought as the mirror rippled and changed. Placing one foot in front of the other, I let the liquid surround me, the feel of it cool against my skin. It didn't take long to get to the other side of the mirror, but for some reason this time the trek was slower than before. Just as I was about to get worried, I heard something.

A voice that I shouldn't be hearing. One that I had only heard in my dreams. The voice of a dead man.

I only heard it once. My name whispered, barely audible, but it was there. I would know that voice anywhere. I stepped out of the mirror and onto the library floor not knowing what to think.

It had been Chess' voice that said my name, clearer than day, and it wasn't likely that I would forget it anytime soon. I couldn't say that it was just my subconscious trying to make me feel better. I couldn't keep making things up to make myself feel better. I told Mab that I was trying to move forward, and that searching for ways to get him back was just a waste of time, but what if I was wrong?

What if Mab had been correct? What if they weren't dead at all and they were just stuck in the Shadow Realm?

I dragged a hand through my blonde hair in frustration. Couldn't things ever be normal? I had enough on my plate; I didn't need my boyfriend haunting me now. Even if it was his voice, and that was a big if, I wouldn't even know how to get to him in the first place.

The only thing I could do was do what I came to do and that included finding the book that Pat had said talked about portals.

If I could figure out how to close the hole in the UnSeelie Court to the Between then maybe there would be something in there about the Shadow Realm, like how the hell I was supposed to get there.

My tennis shoes padded against the tiles of the library floor as I walked through the aisles searching for the section that could possibly have the book Pat had talked about. Phineas Portalus had been the name that he had said, but I had no idea what section I was supposed to look in. As far as I knew, there wasn't a section on portals or about ripping holes in space and time. This wasn't an episode of Doctor Who.

I hadn't been looking long before the voice I dreaded sounded in my ears. "You won't find what you are looking for in here."

Inwardly groaning, I put the book back on the shelf I had been looking at and turned while saying, "Hello, Mother."

My mother, Tatiana, Queen of the Seelie Court, stood at the end of the aisle. Considering her need for attention her outfit today was pretty tame. White pressed pants and a matching suit jacket; the only thing that made me remember this was the Seelie Queen I was dealing with was the lack of clothing beneath the jacket. It was held closed by a tiny bejeweled button, which thankfully kept me from seeing far more of my mother than I wished.

Looking at her made me self-conscious about my own clothing. I wore jeans that had seen better days and a t-shirt that read 'Evil Beware, We Have Waffles'. My enscmble was topped off with beat up tennis shoes. I felt like a street urchin compared to her.

The pinching of her lips told me she wasn't any happier to see me than I was to see her. Which was funny since she hadn't stopped hounding me to talk to her the last few months. If one thing my human and Fae mother had in common it was their persistence to annoy me to death.

"I wasn't expecting you to come in person. I had just sent the message not two hours ago." She crossed her arms over her chest, her brows bunched together in her confusion.

"Message? What message?"

"The one telling you that if you don't contact me, I would be forced to take matters into my own hands, and by that I mean take your friends into my own

69

hands." Her eyes narrowed when I didn't show any recollection of what she was talking about. "Please tell me you received my message? I do so hate to waste a good threat."

"Sorry," I shrugged, "But I'm actually not here for you."

"Really?" her scowl transformed into a curious look that caused her to look younger than she actually was. "Then what, pray tell, are you here wandering the library for? You cannot be homesick already; you wanted to stay in the human world so badly."

The sarcasm in her voice wasn't lost on me, but I chose for once to be the bigger person and ignore her. Instead, I gestured to the books and said, "I'm looking for a way to close the hole to the Between, can't have some unsuspecting Fae wandering in by accident."

"How...noble of you." The way she said it made me feel like she thought less of me for caring, which knowing her, it probably was a fate worse than death.

"Yeah, well, some of us think of others before ourselves. Not something you would likely do on purpose." My mother wasn't a horribly evil person. I had on occasion caught her in a moment of humanity where she couldn't hide how much she cared behind her icy front. Today sadly was not one of those days.

"I care plenty," she waved me off, "I cared enough to come greet you in person rather than sending the guards to apprehend you."

"And why would they do that?"

A slow smile crept up her face that made me want to shiver, but I forced the urge back as she said, "Because you are trespassing of course, and trespassers are killed on sight."

I scoffed at her thinly veiled threat. She didn't want to hurt me; I was the only thing keeping the Council from completely taking her power away from her. If she took me out of the equation than she would be powerless, and there were too many Fae out there with a grudge against her to let that happen.

"You think you are protected because I need you?" she snarled and grabbed my wrist as I picked up another book pretending she didn't bother me. "I made you; I can unmake you just as easily."

71

I glared at her for a moment and then sighed as I dropped my hand. "Can we stop with the soap opera drama, please? I have things to do and places to be. Just tell me what it is you want?"

Her expression was so befuddled by my words I almost thought she hadn't heard me, but then she let go of my wrist and smoothed her hands over her top. "Fine. I wish to go to the human world and the council refuses to let me leave the palace."

"Why would you want to do that?" I couldn't help but laugh.

"The majority of the Fae community has seen fit to live there it is only befitting that I know what they are dealing with."

"Why do you even care? They are out of your hair and somebody else's problem. And by somebody else, I mean me." I turned my attention to scan the shelves once more. It had to be here somewhere.

"That doesn't matter," she said dismissively, "What matters is...what are you looking for?" the tone of her voice made me think she was going to stomp her foot like a child.

"A book by Phineas Portalus and it does matter," I glanced at her from the corner of my eye, "You in the human world would be a disaster. Not to mention, the press would have a field day, and the government is already on my back about Fae registration, they don't need more ammunition to use against us."

"Of all the ridiculous...Fae registration! Really, who do they think they are?" The queen's voice rose until it echoed in the library. "We are immortal and powerful, we don't have to answer to the likes of them. This just proves my point that I should go to the human world and set them straight."

I shook my head furiously. "No, no. Absolutely not. The reason they want to register us is for that very reason. They are afraid of us."

"They should be! What are they compared to us? Insects in the grand scheme of things. They should be bowing to us not the other way around."

"That thinking is precisely my point. You go in there demanding things and they will rise up against us. They have weapons you couldn't even dream of." I knew the humans well, if we tried to take over their land, or make them bow down to us in any way, they would be all over us like a football player at an all you can eat buffet.

"So what? We have magic," she growled, her magic crackling around her, "Their puny metal and plastic cannot compare."

"Not if they drop a nuke on us," I muttered and then said to her, "Look. I have enough to worry about right now without having to babysit you in the human world. Let me deal with this hole first, and then I will talk to the council about it."

At my words, she visibly relaxed. Her face smoothed out and her magic settled back inside of her. "Do you promise?" the uncertainty in her words made me almost guilty that I didn't have any intentions of going to the council, if anything I would tell them to lock her in her room to keep her here. The last thing the human world needed was more Faes, and the Seelie Queen was the Fae of all Faes. Everything they hated about us was solidified into one being and her being there would get us crucified.

Guilty or not, I controlled my scent so she couldn't pick up on my emotions and said, "I promise."

"All right. What were you looking for again?"

I turned back to the shelf so she couldn't see the relief on my face. "A book by Phineas Portalus, supposedly it will tell me how to close the hole."

"Like I said before, you won't find it here."

Huffing an aggravated breath, I spun on her. "Then where is it?"

"Nowhere."

"What do you mean nowhere?"

"Precisely what I said, nowhere." She clucked her tongue at me and then continued, "As in it doesn't exist anymore. I got rid of it a long time ago."

"Why would you do that?" I snarled at her, tired of being here already.

"Oh, don't get so huffy. I couldn't very well let it exist and have someone getting ideas about opening portals between our worlds when I was trying to keep everyone out, now could I?" she shook her head as if I was being silly to even ask.

"Then how the hell am I supposed to close the hole the Shadow man made? It can't just stay there forever. I could just imagine it now, some poor creature would go in thinking it's a great vacation spot and then they wouldn't come back out again."

"I hardly doubt that will be the case, but I can tell you just as easily how to close it as the book would. Dry reading that is." She stared down at her nails with a bored expression on her face.

"Then why didn't you say so in the first place?" I practically shouted at her, my own magic built up in me and began to crackle along my skin.

"You never asked."

CHAPTER

KAT

ONE OF THE first things I had done when Alice had decided to stay in the human world for good was to get her a cell phone. It had been amusing as hell to teach her how to use it. The fact that she could take pictures of herself, message people through text messaging, or even video chat with others was mind-blowing for her. For someone who was used to magic, it was hilarious to see her befuddled expression as she tried to work the device.

Later I regretted it.

She was worse than a teenage girl—always on her phone, texting or taking selfies. She had even figured out how to make a social media profile and had helped a bunch of other Fae get up to date on the human world as well.

"If we want them to accept us as humans we have to act like humans," she had stated when I complained about her phone usage. The phone bill was through the roof, and since she wasn't getting any income, it was all coming out of my pocket. Or rather my parent's pocket. I really did need to talk to someone about getting paid for being the moderator. Even Chess had been getting paid, even if it was through unconventional means.

Surprising even to me there was enough reception in the Underground for me to make a phone call. With Alice on the up and ups of electronic devices, it was easy enough to call her up before I left the library to tell her to meet me at Chess' house. That's why when I stepped through the mirror from the library and onto the purple shag rug of Chess' home; I was surprised that she hadn't made it here yet.

While I waited, I took in the home of my deceased lover. I had only been here once before. Back before I knew who I really was, when everything was new and exciting. Back then, I had been wary of the cat-like human and his flirtatious ways. I would never have thought back then that I would be standing here the way I am now. Or that when I did it would be alone.

My eyes burned at the thought, and I swallowed the lump that had formed in my throat. I forced my feet to move forward to check out the rest of the house. As far as I knew, no one else had been here, but I wanted to be sure no one was squatting in it or desecrating his home.

I cringed at the pink and purple colored furniture as I walked around the living area. The decor still made me feel like a unicorn had barfed all over the place. I guess it was a good thing he was gone, because I knew that there would be some fighting if we had ever gotten a place together. No way in hell would pink ever be on the color pallet.

Moving from the living area, I walked into his bedroom where the door had been thrown open by the shadows. The door still lay open and against the wall, it's hinges barely holding on. I chewed on my lip as I moved further into the room.

I let my hand trail along the comforter on Chess' bed. One that I had never slept in and never would. I picked up his pillow and pressed it to my nose, inhaling deeply. It smelled like him. The hole in my chest ached, and I had the sudden urge to roll around in the bed to engulf myself in his scent.

Before, I could do it, Alice's voice called out, "Lady? Are you here?"

Clearing my throat and placing the pillow back where it belonged, I called back, "I'm in here."

Alice appeared in the doorway with Hatter in tow. Her eyes scanned over me, worry pinching her face. The look in her expression silently asked me if I was all right. All I could do was nod my head as I stepped away from the bed.

"Let's get this over with."

After my mother decided to test my restraint with her dodgy answers, she had finally told me what I needed to know to close the hole. Apparently, it was like any other kind of magic, except that I wouldn't be able to do it alone. The strain on my own magic would be enough that it could kill me, so I would need a conduit to help me focus the power on the task at hand. That was where Alice and Hatter came in. They would act as my hands to help keep the magic in check while I shoved as much force as I could at the sides of the hole. It would be a long and tedious process, but it could be done.

How the hell the Shadow man had done it so easily was beyond my comprehension. Then again, most of the stuff I knew about the shadows was wrong. I wouldn't be surprised to find out that they had survived and were in the Shadow Realm just waiting for their chance to break free once more. Which was all the more reason I needed to figure out how to close the hole so I could get to the Shadow Realm and finish what I started.

"So, this is going to suck," I started as I led them through Chess' home and out of the willow tree.

We stood before the hole, the white of the Between almost blinding in contrast to the rest of the area. Alice stood on one side of me and Hatter on the other. Taking a deep breath, I tried to settle the nerves that had begun to inch up my spine.

"What do you wish of us?" Hatter asked. His gray eyes looked at Alice and then back to me. If he was as nervous as I was he didn't show it. Alice, on the other hand, wrung her hands in front of her not able to hide her feelings as well as her lover.

"I need you guys to help me control my magic while I force the hole to close," I gestured to the edges of the hole in question, "I have enough power to do it on my own but without a buffer of some sort I could get caught up in the magic and drain myself dry."

"It sounds pretty dangerous. Are we sure we want to do this?" Alice asked. Her face filled with apprehension.

Did I want to do it? No. Did I have a choice? Not really. The hole needed to be closed before someone got hurt, and no one else besides Chess and I had enough power to close it. My mother probably could have done it, even Mab, but it would have drained them so much that they wouldn't have recovered. Thus the half-breed had to do it. Wasn't it always that way?

"It'll be fine," I said to Alice, though I could tell by the look she gave me that she knew I was full of shit. I only said things like it'll be fine when I didn't want her to worry, but there wasn't anything I could say to make her feel better. It had to be done, and we were the ones to do it.

"Very well," she sighed and then asked, "What should we do?"

"Just stand there for now. I'm not exactly sure how this will work. In theory, when I start using my magic to close it you need to use your magic to keep mine on target." I explained and then added, "If I start looking like I'm going to go over to the dark side knock me on my ass, got it?"

"With pleasure," Alice replied a bit too happily. The glee in her eyes at the prospect of hitting me was disturbing at best. It made me wonder what kind of person I was living with. Maybe it was time for some roommate therapy.

"Just follow his lead," I pointed to Hatter who I trusted more than Alice not to get me killed. I shook my hands and focused my attention on the hole and then asked, "Ready?"

"As we'll ever be," Hatter's solemn voice replied followed by Alice's gleeful, "Ready!"

"All right, here we go." Even as I said the words my magic began to build up inside me.

It was happy to have a job, joyful even. It had been kept under lock and key too long. In the last six months, there hadn't really been any need for it. The shadows were gone, and I didn't have to use my glamour anymore. Daily activities usually included being a buffer between other Fae and dodging my mothers'. I didn't get a lot of time to practice, nor did I need to use it for household chores. I will admit; I did use it to get the remote when I was too much of a couch potato to get it, but other than that it had been very much kept dormant.

The magic almost knocked me off my feet as it rushed to the surface, and even Alice and Hatter's eyes widened a bit at the force of it. I quickly grabbed a hold of it with my hands, mentally stopping it from flying forward without a purpose. I then directed the magic toward the hole.

In my mind I was taking hold of the edges of the opening, pulling it inward as I imagined what the space should look like with it gone. Thinking about the hole being gone didn't make it so, my magic fought against me, not wanting to do as I asked. I pushed against it, my actual hands coming up in front of me as I tried to push the edges closed.

Beads of sweat dripped down my face and the effort of it made me think that I still needed to join a gym. The muscles in my arms bunched up and burned at the strain the magic was causing as it whipped around in front of us all carefree and defiant. It was like bench-pressing a truck. A truck with a mind of its own and it was saying no way in hell was it touching that hole.

"What's wrong?" Alice finally asked after a few moments. "Why isn't it working?"

"It's being a pissing little shit is what it is," I bit out between clenched teeth. "It's pissed I haven't used it in a while and making me work for it."

"What can we do?" Hatter asked from the corner of my eye.

What could they do? I watched my magic as is swirled and jerked, trying to move any direction but forward. What I needed was a sheep dog that would keep it on the right path, but I would have to settle for the two Fae next to me.

"Use your magic to create a barrier on each side," I started, straining to talk as I fought with my own powers. "This way it will have no choice but to go where I want it to go."

"It shall be so," Hatter answered, his eyes turned to liquid steel as he became focused. He held his hands out on either side of him for what I could only assume was to call his magic, because moments later silver white energy began to flicker along his palms and wrists. His eyes locked with Alice's who had been standing there in awe. "Your turn, dear."

Alice blushed and slowly lifted her hands as well. With more effort than it seemed to take Hatter, Alice concentrated on something off in the distance. Her brow scrunched down, but nothing happened for a moment. Then as if something clicked, a pale blue energy glowed on her palms. Her eyes lit up as she glanced down at the light and then back to Hatter and me.

"I did it!" she cried out with such happiness it made me worry.

"Have you never manifested your magic before?" I asked, trying to keep my focus on the task at hand but worried about her experience in the matter.

"No," she shrugged, "I haven't had the need to, but do not worry, I as the humans say, got this."

My lips pursed at her confidence, not trusting her abilities. Unfortunately, it was too little too late. I didn't have a choice in who helped me, because the magic I had called had to go somewhere and it sure as hell wasn't going back inside of me.

"Fine, follow his lead and no funny business." I nodded to Hatter, the strain of my magic causing my words to sound breathless.

Hatter nodded at Alice and gave her a reassuring smile. "Just watch me."

He lifted his hands until his palms were facing toward where my magic was doing a silly dance regardless of my effort to contain it. Hatter forced the glowing energy from his hands to create a barrier, forcing the green tendrils of magic to move away from his side and come at Alice full force.

She cried out as she quickly put her hands up as well, her magic shoved at mine. Her side wasn't as solid as Hatter's though, and it poked at her trying to find some way out. Thankfully, her barrier held up as well as Hatter's, so it was easy for me to push the magic forward and into the sides of the hole.

Inch by agonizing inch, the hole moved slightly inward, causing Alice to yip, "It's working, Lady! Look!"

"I can see that," I bit out as I struggled to make the hole smaller. Each inch was a battle in itself, and I could feel it in every muscle of my body. Using so much magic, while tiring, was an exhilarating rush. Each pump of magic I pushed out of myself took its place, making me feel full of power. *Invincible.*

The moment the word came to mind I shook my head. No. I couldn't think like that. I had to get this hole closed.

Whenever I became high on magic it meant I was getting close to my limit. The magic wanted to keep going, even if it meant draining my well dry and using my life force in its place. My magic was a double-edged sword. While it could help me in many ways it could also kill me just as easily. Probably why I didn't use it as much as it would like me too.

Finally, the last inch was closed, and I cut my magic off with a sound snap. It fizzled out having lost its purpose but not before lashing out at me and landing me square on my ass.

CHAPTER

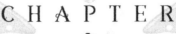

KAT

I DON'T KNOW how space travelers do it. Opening and closing portals between worlds was not easy work.

By the time we got the hole closed my entire body was sticky with sweat from the effort. My whole body ached, and I felt as if I had just run a marathon on one foot. Something that I wouldn't do even if I had ten legs. Running should only be done when someone was chasing you, or when there was a sale on my favorite midnight snack. But not in any circumstance was it done for fun.

"I don't know about you guys," I started bending at the waist as I heaved in in a few breaths. "But I am going to take a hot bath and call it a night."

I turned from the newly closed hole and started back toward the willow, but Alice stopped me with a touch of her hand. In achingly slow motion, I turned my head to raise an eyebrow at her. Ugh. Even that hurt.

"I was wondering," Alice started, her face quickly turning red as she glanced down at the ground and then peeked over her shoulder to where Hatter stood waiting. "If you could maybe..."

One thing most people learn about me quickly was that I was not a pleasant person on the best of days, and when I was tired and disgusting, I had no patience for anyone. So it took all my effort not to shout at Alice for her dallying and to tell her to spit it out already.

"If I could what?"

She shuffled her feet and looked at the ground again, the shy and uncertain Fae was not a side I was used to seeing. She seemed to gather her courage and quickly said, "If you could stay at Chess' tonight so I can be alone with Hatter?"

If I hadn't been listening very closely I would have missed it. Her words came out altogether before she took in a heaving breath and waited for me to answer, anxiety making her form stiff.

Thinking about it for a moment, I didn't know what to say. I mean, I'd had a roommate before; it wasn't uncalled for to ask to have a little privacy with your loved one. A little play action without interruption but what Alice was suggesting wasn't something I had ever planned to do.

"Why can't you go back to his place?" I peered around her to peek at Hatter who seemed to be pretending to not be listening in on our conversation.

"Well, you see the thing is," she giggled wringing her hands nervously. "Hatter kind of has a full house at the moment. There are plenty of Fae who have come over to the human world and those who have gone home to their families. But there are some who have lost family members to the shadows, and they are too scared to go back home, so they have kind of congregated at Hatter's. Making it not really the ideal place to…well you know." She gave me a knowing look.

"Fine. Then I'll just go stay at my mom's," I said moving toward the willow again before her voice stopped me again. "What now?" I spun on my heel and snapped at her.

"I think, I mean," she glanced back to Hatter, "we think it would be good for you, to stay at Chess' place." Alice walked up to me placing her hands on my shoulders. "Don't pretend like we haven't noticed you dragging through life. You don't sleep well, and the only time you visit Chess' grave is when you can't stand the ache you feel in here." She poked the middle of my chest where the hole pulsated at the mention of it.

"I don't know what you are talking about," I muttered looking away from her and to the ground. "I'm fine."

"The heart is not so easily healed or so easily hidden away just because we wish it to be so." My eyes darted over to where Hatter stood, his arms over his chest as he nodded solemnly. I didn't know what to say. His words rang true for me but at the same time, I didn't want to admit them, especially since I had just recently heard Chess' voice when passing through the mirror. I suspected mentioning it now would not do my case any good.

"Why don't you stay here tonight?" Alice suggested again. "It might do you some good. Help you to move on."

"You know Mab says they aren't really dead." I couldn't help but bring up. I wasn't the only one who couldn't let go and try as I might to move on, the damn cat kept bringing me back in.

Alice pursed her lips not happy with my words. "She's a grieving mother. Of course she would hold on just as much as you would, but Lady...Katherine," she shook her head sadly her blonde hair whipping around her, "they're gone. They aren't coming back, no matter how much you want it. So why don't you take a bath and have a good cry and then in the morning you will feel better. I promise." She gave me an encouraging smile that I only half returned.

"If you say so."

"I know so."

AFTER ALICE AND Hatter left to have their little night in, I waited around outside of the willow. I was delaying the inevitable, I knew that, but going back in there was too hard for me to handle after I used so much energy. Happily in denial, I moved over to Chess' original throne, the vines on it were wilted and dried, unlike the beautiful ones that had covered it the first time I had been here. Things had changed so much since then.

It was hard to believe not even a year ago I was a smart mouthed human thinking I knew everything while making my way through what I thought was Wonderland. Now, here I was a half-blood and the Seelie Princess to boot. I scrubbed a hand over my face and let out a bitter laugh. All I had wanted back then was to get home and away from that perverted cat, and now I would give anything to have him here again. Maybe Alice was right. I needed to surround myself with Chess' stuff so I could finally let him go.

Not able to convince myself to delay any longer, I moved toward the entry to the willow tree. Placing my hand on the bark, I let myself be enveloped in the magic of the tree. Stepping through the bark and onto the lush unicorn barf carpet, I let out a deep sigh. I wondered if he had any food around here, and if so, was it any good anymore?

I maneuvered around Chess' house searching for the kitchen and something to fill my empty stomach. Who knew closing tears between worlds would make one so hungry? I'd have to remember that for the next time it happened. I just hoped there wasn't a next time.

As luck would have it there was some food still in the kitchen. Some weird prepackaged food that didn't have an expiration date but was similar enough to chips that I decided to chance it.

Lounging on one of the fur covered chairs; I munched on my snack and tried not to go cross-eyed from the decor. What exactly was I supposed to do now? It wasn't like he had a television set or any books that I could see. How exactly did he stay entertained here?

The last thought made me pause. Oh yeah. I frowned hard. I had forgotten what Chess' extracurricular activities included before he met me. Before he became my

Chess he was little more than a man whore, taking on male and female Fae alike as payment for his service to the crown. Just thinking about it made me sick to my stomach.

My eyes moved toward the bedroom door where the bed was visible from my seat. Had he taken them there? How many had he had in his bed? A large lump filled my throat and I fought to swallow it as I shook my head. No. Don't think like that. I didn't want to remember him as a certifiable prostitute. He wasn't like that with me. He was funny and kind. Even when he was supposed to be working for my mother he had always put my wants and needs first. It was one of the reasons I had fallen for him so easily.

Dusting my hands off, I stood from the chair and moved to the bedroom. Bypassing the bed with a sideways glance, I beelined it for the bathroom. I opened the door and closed it behind me; even though I was the only one here I still didn't want to take any chances. People could still come and go as they pleased here. The last thing I wanted was to be caught naked by a stranger; it was bad enough Alice didn't understand the meaning of the word privacy.

As soon as the door was closed behind me, my eyes went straight to the claw foot tub. I let out a longing sigh. Chess had a bathtub I could only dream about. The one at my grandmother's house was a standard tub that barely let me fill it up enough to cover my boobs and that was only if I was laying down flat. This tub, though, I could easily sit up on the side and have a nice luxurious bath fully covered and all. Just the thought of it made me relax a bit.

Wasting no time at all, I quickly stripped off my sweaty clothing and turned the water on. Once it was good and full I stepped in and sank down until I was covered to my neck. God, why hadn't I done this before? The freaking cat had been holding out on me.

Thinking of Chess made me wish he were here now. He would know how to make this bath worthwhile. My face and chest heated up at all the things he would do to me if he were here now. I sighed deeply and sank even further into the tub. Look at me. I was supposed to be getting over Chess and moving on but everything here just made me think of him and thus miss him even more. Maybe this was a bad idea.

I climbed out of the tub and wrapped a towel around myself and then grabbed another to dry my hair. I couldn't even enjoy soaking in the tub. I pulled out my cell phone to see that I had almost no battery left and no bars. So much for having some form of entertainment.

I growled in frustration, and I stared at myself in the mirror. What was I supposed to do now? It was too early to go to bed, but after the day I had, it wouldn't hurt to call it a night already. Besides, the sooner I went to bed the sooner I could get out of here and go home.

Marching into the bedroom, I started for the closet. Chess and I weren't even close to the same size, but he had to have something I could wear. I so wasn't putting my sweaty clothes back on.

Opening the closet door, I smiled slightly at the sight before me. Who had or needed so many clothes? I swore he was worse than my sister. I could count on one hand how many pairs of shoes I had and he had at least two dozen. Not to mention, all the different pants and tops he had organized by color. Even dead I was learning things about him. I wouldn't have pegged him for OCD. Giggling, I thumbed through his clothing. The whole closet smelled of him, a sort of spicy scent that filled my nose and made my heart ache.

Not able to stand to be in here for one moment longer, I grabbed the first shirt I found and darted out of the room. I looked down at what I had grabbed, a sheer crop top that wouldn't cover half of my bust let alone work as a nightshirt. Shaking my head, I went back into the closet, this time taking the time to grab a half decent shirt.

Walking out of the closet, I pulled the tank top over my head. If Chess was still alive, and I somehow magically got him back, we were going to have to talk about what regular everyday clothing looked like. While looking at him prance around in tight pants and chest-baring shirts was enjoyable, it wasn't really good for functioning in the human world.

I moved over to the bed and hesitated. Placing my hand on the top of the comforter, I frowned. Just a few hours ago I had been thinking how I would never lay in this bed but now here I was getting ready to slip underneath the covers. Trying not to think about it too much, I climbed beneath the comforter and laid my head back onto the pillow. I turned over and buried my face into the pillow. I could smell the cat here too. With the pillow clutched close to my face, I fell into a restless sleep, staring twins and a dark haired woman with way too much makeup on.

CHAPTER

CHESS

ON THE POSITIVE side, dinner with the twins wasn't as bad as I thought it would be. They kept the conversation light and mainly spent the whole time flirting with Morgana, an attraction I couldn't understand. Did they not know how atrocious she was?

Thankfully, the dinner didn't last long and we were on the move again. I was surprised I didn't have to let my claws out when it was time to leave. The twins had begged us to stay the night, and when I say us, I mean her. They couldn't give two licks about me.

Morgana, though, laughed them off with a promise to stay on the way back after she got rid of her extra baggage. She looked to me as she said it, and I had the childish urge to stick my tongue out at her. I resisted the urge and waited like a patient dog for her to lead on.

Walking through the fog had become more of an inconvenience now. I followed after her, not too worried about where we were going or how we got there. I just wanted to get to the Reaper and get home. The more questions I asked the longer it would take, and I didn't have any desire to stay longer than I already had.

"You are being awfully quiet back there," Morgana finally broke the silence between us. "I would think you'd be talking off my ear now that we don't have the twins to intimidate you."

I scoffed, "They don't bother me."

"Really?" she glanced over her shoulder, quirking an eyebrow. "That's not what I got from how tense you were at dinner."

"Can you blame me for wanting to get a move on? The more time we waste with your lovers the longer it will take me to get out of here."

"Jealous?"

"Hardly," I laughed.

Morgana made a humph sound and turned back around, putting her nose in the air. After that, we went back to silence, which I preferred, to be honest. I liked someone who gave me a challenge and could hold their own as much as the next fellow but after a while it just got tiring.

"Here we are," she said when she finally stopped to talk to me again. We exited the fog and entered another mirror graveyard like area, practically identical to hers and the twins, it didn't make me feel any closer to getting to the Reaper and out of here.

"Is the Reaper here?" I asked moving around her to scan the area. I didn't see anything that could be remotely what we were looking for and spun back around to wait for her answer.

"No, not here." She smiled up at me expectantly as if there was a joke I was supposed to be in on.

"Then what are we here for?" I growled at her but all she did was giggle and point a finger behind me.

"Him."

I hadn't seen my dad in centuries. He looked exactly how I remembered him.

He was an large cat about the size of a tiger with fur stripped like mine, a pink base with purple stripes. He had huge emerald green eyes and a face full of sharp teeth. Lounging on top of the rock, his tail wrapped around his hind legs, moving up and down with interest.

For a moment I thought he wouldn't recognize me. I'd been nothing more than a boy when he died. Would he recognize me as a man?

Morgana sashayed right over to him without a care in the world. It was strange how even though she was wearing casual clothing she still moved as if she were dressed in fine satin and jewels. It was the kind of attitude that came from growing up in royalty. It made me wonder exactly who she really was.

"Cheshire," she purred, her hand coming out to stroke the top of my father's head. I half expected him to growl and nip at her, but he angled his head further into her hand, silently requesting a scratch. Granting his request, her fingers dug into the fur behind his ears, causing the large feline to purr with contentment.

After a few moments, I was beginning to feel awkward. The scratching had gone on longer than was appropriate in polite society and made me wonder if they knew each other better than they appeared.

I cleared my throat causing Morgana's hand to stop and my father's eyes to open. The look in his eyes had he been one with physical magic would have decimated me on the spot. Luckily for me, I got my ability to phase between the realms from him. It was the only true power he had besides his massive size.

"As weird as this is turning out to be, could you stop with the petting and explain to me why we are here?" I gestured around the hovel like area, not much different than Morgana's, except his mirror graveyard only held a few mirrors as opposed to the dozen or so that filled Morgana's.

"Always the petulant child. I see after all these centuries you have not changed," my father's voice boomed out of his chest.

Shrugging, I gave him my best fang-toothed grin. "What can I say, I take after my father." Even as the words fell from my lips I knew they were only partly true.

There were many things about myself that had nothing to do with my father. Things that I hoped hadn't come from my mother. The fact that I could easily let myself be convinced to make Kat fall for me for the queen's plan. Or the fact that I had been so cowardice and unable to tell her no when she kept forcing her people onto me. Now that I knew what real love felt like, I felt that my father never loved me, and if my mother even had a chance to be with me, she probably hadn't either.

"Like father like son," Morgana laughed, the back of her hand covering her mouth, "I knew bringing you here would be interesting."

"Is that all this is for you? A new source of entertainment?" I growled at her, the smirk on her face at my outrage caused my anger to quicken. "I trusted you to lead me to the Reaper not drag me all over the Shadow Realm so you can get your kicks off my family drama. And you," I pointed a clawed finger at my father, "you are a shape shifter, why must you stay in animal form? You know how that makes me feel!"

My father cocked his head to the side, curiosity in his gaze, and then he nodded his head. "I apologize. I did not realize at your age you still had insecurities about your form."

Troll malarkey. He knew well and good I still had hang ups on my form. As half UnSeelie and half Seelie, I didn't have the full powers of either parent. While my mother had been able to transport from one place to the other with a single thought, so much so she could go between worlds. I, on the other hand, could only go small distances and only if I had been there before. My father as he so dutifully pointed out could shapeshift between a large cat form and a Fae form that he used to mate with my mother. He told me once that he preferred the cat form because it was simpler; his mind didn't have to focus on things he couldn't control as much. I used to envy him but after a while, I realized I would never be like him. Always stuck in between forms, I began to resent it.

I tried not to let my interest show but as usual when he shapeshifted my eyes were drawn to his form. His whole body enveloped in light, his form shrank down from the massive cat into that of a man. The fur on his skin receded, his jaw shortened and his paws lengthened into hands and feet. Long, dark purple hair hung from his head and brushed the ground below. The only part of him giving anyone any clue of what he once was were the sharpened canines in his mouth and claws on his hands. Unlike me, he didn't have ears on his head but pointed human ears, something else I would never achieve without glamour.

Unfortunately, with his transformation also came the lack of clothing, something that Morgana had no problem with as her eyes trailed my father's figure with a hunger I'd never seen on her face. I wasn't a prude by any means but seeing her watch my father that way made me a bit queasy.

"Clothing please," I croaked out as he stood to his full height, showing off that I did indeed gain some attributes from him. His lips twisted downward as he walked into the hovel near us.

"Well, this certainly is interesting," Morgana murmured, her eyes on the door my father had just exited. I didn't answer her and turned away to look at the mirrors around us. I was curious to see if they showed the same as Morgana's or if it was different for each person. If it was specific to each person's past, then I was curious to know why the mirrors in Morgana's area showed Kat's house.

Kneeling down by a mirror close to me, I placed my hand on the surface. This one rippled and stirred and before long the reflection was no longer showing me and the darkness behind, but the inside of my bedroom. Frowning hard, I removed my hand from it. I moved to another mirror and touched it as well, this time it showed me my bathroom and in the reflection was Kat.

"Kat! Katherine!" I cried out gripping the edges of the mirror as my eyes widened. What was she doing in my bathroom? She had just been home not too long ago. The mirror only allowed me to see her from her collarbone and up, since she had bare shoulders and dripping hair I could only assume she had just gotten out of my bath. The thought of her in my home warmed my heart but at the same time made me ache to be home. I wanted to be the one to show her around. Before she had only been there long enough to change and then she had to take off before the shadows got her. The aspect of having her in my bed was too much for me to contemplate.

Before my thoughts could wander into even more dangerous territory so close to Morgana and my father, she leaned in close to the mirror as if she was looking right at me.

"I'm here. I'm right here." I shook the mirror's frame and growled out in frustration when she simply dried her hair and then moved out of the frame. Throwing myself away from the mirror, I collapsed in a huff on the ground. She was in the Underground that should mean I had a better chance to get a hold of her, but it didn't seem like it was going to happen.

"Is that your mate?" my father's voice sounded from behind me, but I didn't look up at him as I stared hard at the ground. When I didn't answer he kept talking, the guy was as bad as I was when it came to taking a hint. "She is very pretty."

Morgana made a disgusted noise in the back of her throat that caused me to glare at her, daring her to say something bad about Kat. I might be stuck here, but I wasn't about to let her dishonor my woman.

111

At my intense glare, she promptly closed her mouth and turned her eyes from me. Smart woman.

"Your mother was pretty like that," my father continued as if I wasn't ignoring him.

"I wouldn't know." I wrapped my arms around my knees laying my cheek on the top of one knee. "Kat is my mate, or she would be if I wasn't stuck here."

From the corner of my eye I saw him nod his head before sitting down on the ground beside me. He had found some clothing, thankfully. A plain pair of pants and dark tunic. Not something I would have ever picked but it was better than having to stare at his genitals the entire time.

"You know, prior to what you may believe, your mother and I weren't forced into mating." My head jerked up as he spoke, suspicion on my face. "Your mother was quite beautiful, and I was young and naive. All I wanted to do was rut and your mother was prime for the taking."

My face twisted in disgust at the imagery, but I waited for him to continue whatever it was he seemed to need to say to me.

"It was only by luck that we fell in love." There was a soft smile on his face as he talked about her that I had never seen before.

"So, what happened? Why did you two break up and then leave me?" I couldn't help the words that flew from my mouth. I had the chance to ask all the questions I had ever wanted to say, and the child that wanted his parents needed the answers.

"What always happens in the Underground," my father sighed when I gave him a confused look, "the queen got involved."

Ah, yes. The Seelie Queen was a right bitch, and it wasn't at all surprising that she had ruined not just her own daughter's life but all those around her. I really hoped Kat gave her a harsh punishment for her crimes.

"In any case, I know what you are going through." He patted me on the arm in a fatherly gestured he had never shown me in my childhood. "I still feel like a piece of me is missing now that I'm stuck here and she is the Reaper only knows where."

I shook his hand off. "But it's not like there is a piece of me missing, there *is* a piece of me missing."

"I know it must feel like it but after a while, it won't be so bad," he tried to reason with me, but I stood to my feet.

"No, it's you who doesn't understand. We are linked by magic. I was thrown to the Bandersnatch and she saved me. Our magic, her magic is inside of me and each day we are apart it's like I'm dying inside." I gripped my chest where the hole in my heart sat, just talking about it made my throat clog up with emotion.

My father's eyes widened at my story and even Morgana's mouth dropped open in surprise. "I'm sorry," he shook his head sadly, his hair swinging around him, "I wasn't aware. I've heard of Fae who have shared magic before but never have I met someone who knew what it was like. Being here must be more than torture for you."

"You can't even imagine."

There was an awkward silence for a few moments; my father's gaze stared hard at the mirrors around us. Then without warning, he slapped his thighs and stood to his feet. "Well, then we have to get you out of here."

"How are we going to do that?" I followed behind him as he moved from where we had been sitting to the mirror that had shown me Kat in the bathroom. My eyes traced his every movement as he pressed his hand to the mirror's surface. This time the mirror didn't show the bathroom but somewhere I had only seen once before. It was a place that I kept pushed far to the back of my mind because if I thought too much about it I would run screaming into the night and never regain my sanity.

The Bandersnatch.

The image was blurry, but I could vaguely make out the form of a crouched woman, curled up into a ball against a wall. Her body shook as her arms gripped her knees tightly to her face. The faces that taunted and tormented me were circling around her giving her her daily dose of guilt and dismay. The woman glanced up briefly as if she could tell we were watching her and my breathing froze.

"Is that?" I started and my father traced the surface with his hand, a sad expression on his face.

"Your mother? Yes." He sighed and removed his hand turning back to me. "The mirrors show you what you want to see most. I watched you grow up even as you were twisted up in the queen's lies. I'd rather watch your life than watch her suffer, though it pains me to do so."

I wanted to tell him I knew where she was but even if I could get out of here and get to her, there was no telling what kind of condition she'd be in. Kat had barely been able to bring me back to normal after only being there for a few days let alone the years my mother had been in there being feasted on by the Bandersnatch. Telling him would only make him suffer more.

"Not to be insensitive, but what does this have to do with me getting out of here?" I walked over to his side staring at the reflection of us side by side. Father and son. Both separated from their loves, both broken beyond repair. It was a sad state we were in.

This time my father's lips curved into a smile as he clasped me on the shoulder. "We, my son, are going to get a message to your mate. If she was able to share her magic with you, then you are connected, and she will be able to find you."

Sending a message to Kat seemed too good to be true. Even if we could pull it off I worried whether or not she would believe it was from me and not a trick. Could Kat put aside her grief long enough to figure it out?

CHAPTER

KAT

I AWOKE FROM my dream with a jerk. The twins I had been dreaming about had quickly morphed into a laughing cat as big as a house. Its large paws swiping out at me had tossed me from the dream.

I rubbed my eyes with the palm of my hand before peeking out at the darkened room. A quick glance at my, somehow miraculously not dead phone, told me it was just after one a.m. and I should not be awake. But something had caused it and if I knew anything about the Underground, it was usually best to follow the warning.

Slipping out of bed, I padded across the floor and into the bathroom. I covered my mouth as I started to yawn but then promptly choked.

The mirror in the bathroom, that shouldn't have still been fogged up from the bath I had taken hours ago, was covered with a white film. It wasn't the lack of heat in the room causing it that worried me it was what was written there in the fog.

Kitten.

In loopy letters that could only belong to one person. I shook my head and rubbed eyes once more. I had to be dreaming. That was it. I was still in bed and this was all a dream. It's happened before why shouldn't it happen again?

A stinging pain radiated through my arms as I pinched myself. I looked back to the mirror. Nope, it was still there. As clear as day. One word that I knew without a doubt had come from Cheshire S. Cat.

He was the only one with the balls to call me kitten. The only one that I allowed to give me such ridiculous pet names. And the only one who would leave a message on the mirror in his own home for me to find.

Inching closer to the mirror, I peered into the surface. Though fogged over from the nonexistent steam, it wasn't hard to tell that there was nothing in the mirror but my own smeared reflection. Reaching up, I swiped my hand across the surface, half of me upset that I had destroyed his message, but the other part more anxious to see what was hidden.

Unfortunately, there wasn't anything more to see. The only thing looking back at me was my wide-eyed exhausted face. Frowning, I placed my hand on the frame of the mirror hoping that it might be connected like the rest.

When nothing happened after a few moments, I dropped my hand to my side with a frustrated huff. Chewing on my bottom lip, I furrowed my brows while staring hard at the mirror, trying to think of a way to show myself some kind of sign that I wasn't crazy. That Chess really was trying to get through to me.

Realization dawned on me. The mirror might not be connected on this side. For how pervy Chess was it was pretty hilarious that he didn't want anyone peeping in on him while he was bathing. Not that I could blame him, his kind of tub was meant for relaxation, not naughty fun time. Though, if Chess was here I wouldn't exactly tell him no.

The thought of calling Pat to activate the mirror seemed like a bad idea. He wasn't exactly helpful these days, even though he had pointed me to the book on portals. But something inside of me told me I was barking up the wrong Fae.

I shouldn't need his help anyways. Was I the Seelie Princess, or wasn't I? I was supposed to be all powerful, right? That meant I shouldn't need his help. I should be able to do it myself. That's if I didn't kill myself in the process.

Shaking the nerves out of my hands, I drew my shoulders back and placed my hands on either side of the mirror. Closing my eyes, I dug deep inside for my magic and coaxed it awake. It responded lazily and aggravated. It wasn't happy that I wanted to use it again after exerting so much energy on closing the hole. I mentally apologized, hoping it would feel my desperation to get through the mirror.

It seemed to think on it for a moment but then consented and came to the surface. I took the magic and focused it on the frame of the mirror, envisioning Chess. I didn't know where he was, so I couldn't think of the place only him.

I pictured his long pink hair trailing over his shoulders as it brushed his chest. His emerald green eyes that always drew me in and left me breathless. Even that smirk of his that half made me want to hit him and the other half kiss him. All the little things that made up my love for Cheshire S. Cat were funneled into the mirror.

I held my breath as I watched the mirror shake and glow. It had never done that before. Stepping back from the sink, my eyes grew wider and wider until I felt as if they might pop out of their sockets. When the glow faded it wasn't my face looking back at me, but Chess'. Well, Chess and someone that looked so much like him he had to be related.

My heart stopped and my breath caught as I moved slowly toward the mirror. I reached out with my hand. My lip quivered and my eyes burned as my fingers touched the glass surface where his face was. The expression on his face matched mine, a bit in wonder and disbelief but there was one thing on his face that wasn't on mine.

Surprise.

His eyes flickered to where my hand sat on the mirror. He slowly raised his own hand until it lined up with mine. Chess' hand was larger than mine, his fingertips stretching out several inches past where my fingers ended. For a moment, I swore I could feel him. The hole in my chest pulsated and a smile crept up my face as I laughed.

"H...how? How is this possible?" My eyes snapped to his emerald orbs that were just as engulfed with emotion as mine. Then they turned to the man by his side. "You? You did this?" I asked, my gaze following Chess' to the man beside him.

A sad smile was my response and with a shake of his head he said, "No, this is both of you."

"What do you mean?" I locked eyes with Chess once more, the fact that he was actually here before me was still hard to believe.

"You are connected, that is the only way the barrier between the Shadow Realm and your world can work. Two of one heart can do more than even the Reaper himself can conspire."

"So, you are in the Shadow Realm?" I cut in trying to see behind the two images in the mirror to the barren area behind him.

Before either of them could answer, a feminine hand with nails painted as red as blood slipped over Chess' shoulder. The dark haired woman from my dream moved into the frame. She pressed her front firmly against Chess' back. The animalistic urge to rip her off him gnawed at me so strong that it took all my will to not throw myself at the mirror.

"Yes, he has," the woman's deep sultry voice slid out of her mouth. She stroked a hand along Chess' shoulder, her lips curled up in a shit eating grin, "but don't worry I've kept him company so he would not be alone."

I was two seconds away from giving her a bitch please speech when in the blink of an eye Chess shoved her away and out of the frame. Her cries of outrage rang in my ears and I flicked Chess a look.

"Friend of yours?" I cocked my head to the side, lips pursed.

"Hardly." The complete disdain in his voice when he said the word made me fall for him all over again.

"After all I've done for you," the woman screeched off to the side, which caused Chess to roll his eyes, a move that was something he had to have gotten from me. "I hope the Reaper damns you both, you ungrateful brat."

"The Reaper?" That was the second time they had mentioned the Reaper in the span of five minutes. The likelihood that it was a coincidence was spotty at best.

"Speaking of the Reaper," the man that looked so much like Chess it was uncanny said. "He is more than likely on his way now. A hole like this one wouldn't escape his notice. So, I suggest you say what you have to say and quickly."

"Who are you?" I started, but Chess cut me off this time.

"He's my father." My gaze jerked to his and then back to the man. It all made sense. The coloring, the line of his jaw, even the twinkle in his eye was unmistakably Cheshire S. Cat.

"Your father," I choked out, the original Cheshire was standing right before me.

The one from the stories of Alice in Wonderland, but this was one version of him that I had never seen before. The Cheshire cat from the stories was exactly that, a cat. But this guy could have been a movie star or runway model. Or some famous cosplayer.

"Yes, and he's right. We don't have time to explain everything, no matter how much I'd love to sit here just talking to you, love." He gave me a fanged-toothed grin that made my heart ache to hold him. "You can get me out, pet. We can be together again."

I shook my head. "But how? I don't know how to get to you or where you even are?" I tried once again to make out more of the background but unfortunately, with them standing in the way, I couldn't make out more than a darkened sky and dirt floors.

"If you are connected as my son has stated then it will lead you to where you need to be." His words were ominous even while they were supposed to be hopeful. Yep, he was definitely related to Chess. Riddles were great for party tricks but a map would be more useful.

Before I could ask another question or to even say goodbye both of their heads jerked toward a sound I couldn't hear and then the mirror cleared showing me my own face once more.

"No!" I slammed my hands on the porcelain sink causing it to creak beneath my palms. When the mirror still did not give me the image of Chess back, I reached up and shook the frame as hard as I could, screaming at the top of my lungs but still nothing.

Seething at my lack of response, I reached for my magic and found the well not surprisingly, resistant. I hadn't been very nice with how I used it recently. First with the hole and then the mirror, now it was telling me no more. It didn't surprise me; my magic's personality was as difficult as my own. Which meant I was out of luck and out of ideas.

How the hell was I supposed to find Chess when I didn't know where to start? Chess' father said that if we were connected then it would lead me to them. I could only assume by connected he meant by the magical bond we shared, a bond that had given me nothing but heartache the last six months. One that for once might help me now.

Taking a deep breath in and then letting it out, I tried to calm the torrent of emotion that raged inside of me. If I was going to figure out where the hell I was going I couldn't be dwelling on trying to contact him again.

What I needed to do was find someone who knew more about the Shadow Realm than I did. There were two people who knew more than I did. My mother and Mab. Since one wasn't someone I wanted to talk to, and the other had been trying to persuade me to go after them in the first place, it looked like I was headed for the UnSeelie Palace. I had some groveling to do.

Oh, joy.

CHAPTER

CHESS

"YOU REALLY SHOULDN'T have done that."

I didn't have to look behind me to know who had spoken. The chill that went down my spine, the fear that made its way into my heart was easy enough to pinpoint down the cause.

The Reaper.

There wasn't much information available on the Reaper. Many of the Fae pretended like he didn't even exist. That he was just a made up story meant to scare you into behaving. But I knew the Reaper was very much real.

When I was a child, not much more than a Faeling, I had thought I was big and brave. That I didn't need anyone and could face anything on my own. That was shortly after my father had left me and I was left all on my own.

I'd been warned about the Veil of the Faeries before. That going there would only cause trouble. But I was young and naive. I wanted to see the faeries, and nobody was going to tell me otherwise.

What no one thought to tell me was that the reason people stayed away from the Veil was because that was where the Reaper came to collect the souls of the Fae who had passed on. So, there I was no more than a babe, searching high and low for a faerie to take home with me. But even the faeries weren't stupid enough to come out to play when the reaper visited. I'd had the bad luck of having my adventure on that day.

When the Reaper was in your presence the air grew cold and the hairs on the back of your neck stood at attention. It was like that now, and unlike then I couldn't run home and hide under the covers hoping he wouldn't come for me. No, this time, I had to turn and face him like a man. Because if anyone was getting me out of the Shadow Realm it was him.

"And why is that?" I slowly turned from the mirror to look upon a Fae's worse nightmare. What I saw was pretty disappointing, to be honest.

He had a black billowy cloak that hung around his shoulders, his hood was pushed back to show not a skeletal head or decaying corpse, but that of a normal man. His long black hair lay across his shoulders and upper chest. His eyes were a dark blue that had I been interested in dating anyone I would have turned on my charm.

But there was something about the Reaper. Something familiar that didn't set right. Whether it was the line of his jaw or the scowl on his lips, I didn't know, but I had met this man before.

"You give her false hope and the Fae need her now. More than you." The Reaper's voice was fluid like silk sheets and harsh like nails at the same time.

"She won't stop looking for me," I stated, putting my nose in the air. "Now that she knows I'm alive. She'll come for me."

"And had you been patient you would have found your own way out but just like the rest of them you are impatient and too wrapped up in your wants and needs to see the bigger picture." His words snapped at me and made me cringe. Shame filled me.

I had only been thinking of myself and getting home. Yes, the hole in my heart hurt. It felt like every second, every breath was pulling at the edges of the hole making it bigger and bigger until I felt like it might swallow me whole. It never did, though.

"It's too late now." I gulped and brushed my hair over my shoulder. I waited for him to scowl at me more, or better yet to kill me on the spot, but he did worse. He took one look at me and threw his head back and laughed.

"So much like your father, you are," he patted me on the shoulder; the feel of it caused a chill to run through me. "Come, let's walk."

I looked to my father who had since changed back to his feline form. A coward if I ever saw one. Morgana stood to the side watching on with amusement in her eyes but also a hint of fear. Interesting.

The Reaper spun on his heel, his cloak sweeping the floor behind him. I hesitated for just a moment; long enough to send a questioning look to my father who gave me a very feline answer, his ears switched. I now knew how Kat felt about those kinds of answers. She referred to them as irritating non-fucking answers.

With no other choice but to stay with the one who had obviously checked out, and the other who I'd already pissed off, or to follow him I quickly caught up to where he was moving into the fog.

Like with Morgana, the fog just seemed to clear for him as she moved through it allowing me to follow after. Did the claims Morgana had to queendom actually ring true? Or was anyone that was supposed to be here able to move between hovels at will? They were questions that could only be answered by asking them, but I didn't think the Reaper was in much of a giving mood.

"Only the certain few, myself included," the Reaper said out of the blue answering my question. Had he read my mind? "Yes, I did," he answered again and then smirked over his shoulder at me. "A perk of being the Reaper."

"The Reaper?" I cocked my head at him, "so it is a title? Not your name?"

He shook his head. "You should know good and well that names hold power and in my case, the title the Reaper holds more power than something as plain and ordinary as Eugene."

I forced myself not to bust out laughing, though my lips ticked at the name. I shook my head in an effort to cover up my laughter. "I could see how that would be a problem."

"Thus, the Reaper was born." He spread his arms out wide around him making the fog where his arms touched diminish. "Though, I can't take full claim for such a name since I am not the first nor will I be the last Reaper. I am simply surviving my time until another takes my place."

As he finished his explanation the fog dispersed around us, the ground turned from the dead grass I craved to gray stone. He led me along a stone path lined by the first water I had seen since being here that hadn't come out of a faucet. The water was dark except for the swirling tendrils of blue energy moving through it.

A sudden urge to lean down and try to scoop one out came over me. Literally, like a cat with a string, my eyes followed the glowing lights as they came closer and closer to me. They were almost just in reach when a hand clasped down on my shoulder and jerked me back.

My wide eyes locked onto the Reaper's. What just happened? I looked down at where I was standing, just an inch away from the edge, which was two feet farther than I had been before. I didn't even remember moving.

"You don't want to be doing that, trust me." He patted me on the shoulder and continued toward a large stone building. Large columns held up the roof, which had carvings of ancient times that I couldn't quite remember the stories to.

Turning my gaze from the decor, I stared at the Reaper's back. "What just happened? What are those things?"

"Those," he said over his shoulder, gesturing a hand toward the swirling blue lights that even at just a glance coaxed me to come closer. "Are the souls of the dead. If you touch them they'll latch onto and suck you of your magic."

"Wait a moment," I said catching up to him, "I thought this wasn't the afterlife? Morgana said I wasn't dead, but if those are the dead then how am I here? How are any of them here?"

"She's right, in a way," he waved a finger in the air as he talked, "you aren't dead, and the rest aren't really dead either but they," he pointed to the spirits in the water, "are most certainly dead."

"No offense meant, but that didn't exactly answer my question."

He threw his head back and laughed. "No, I suppose it didn't." He made a humming noise, as he seemed to think on what to say next. "You see the Seelie Queen and I have an arrangement of sorts."

I snorted. "I heard all about that, it's the reason the shadows were made in the first place. That arrangement caused more Fae to die in the last year than I'd ever heard of in my whole life."

The Reaper stopped abruptly, and I almost walked into his back before he spun on me. His eyes were electric blue and would have shot a bolt of lightning straight into me had he had the chance.

"You, half-blood, do not know what you speak of. We did what we thought was best for our kind," he hissed at me, his anger palpable in the air. "What you call a lot of

Fae would have been much worse had we let those who became the shadows stay in your realm. Count yourself luck."

With those words he turned away, marching toward the looming building before us. I let out a breath I hadn't realized I had been holding and frowned. There seemed to be more to the story than Kat or I had ever known. His words didn't make the deaths of my fellow Fae any less meaningful, but the fact that it could have been worse than it was caused a shiver down my spine.

"Are you coming?" my eyes shot up to where the Reaper was waiting for me at the steps of the entrance.

"Yes, yes," I called out hurrying my footsteps to catch up to him. "I apologize, it seems that I have been left in the dark on some aspects of our fallen foe."

"As you should be," he replied before his face fell and his eyes glanced toward the inside, "but not so fallen as you expect."

I was confused at first by his words but then when what he said made sense in my mind, my heart stopped. What he said couldn't be true. The spell that Kat did that caused me to end up here had worked, hadn't it? But then it had only said it would send the shadows back to where they belonged; it didn't say anything about killing them.

"Where are they?" I asked, my teeth clenched until the muscle in my jaw burned.

"Come, this way." He opened a large door made of the same stone that the walls and roof were made of, and his arm gestured me inside.

I raised my brow and moved past him and into the building. The floors were stone throughout, the large columns outside also resided on the inside, the only difference was on every column mounted on the wall were torches of blue light. Normally, I would make a joke about him having a thing for blue, but in this case I felt that my comment might be ill-mannered toward someone who had my fate in their hands.

As I walked further into the area that was larger than even the Seelie Queen's ballroom, I felt the distinct presence of the Reaper at my back. Each step I took felt as if I was heading toward something. Something dark and evil, something I never wanted to feel again. Then my eyes landed on the pedestal at the head of the room. My mouth went dry as I took in the form lying on the slab of stone.

The UnSeelie Prince. The last host of the Shadows and Kat's ex-fiancé. If I were smart I would walk out the door and leave whatever was going on with him alone. But call me a masochist, or maybe I had turned into a good guy, but I had an overwhelming urge to find out what would happen to him.

I approached the slab, my eyes roaming over his form. He was still clad in the clothing I had seen him in last: dark pants and an even darker shirt. They were his signature clothing that he thought made him look powerful, but I had always thought it just washed him out. He looked as if he was sleeping, but his skin was deathly pale, the veins underneath his skin pulsated with darkness. A blue power enveloped him in a sort of barrier that I was hesitant to touch.

"It won't hurt you," the Reaper's voice behind, and much to my chagrin, made me jump. "It is just keeping him in a comatose state."

"What's wrong with him?" My eyes stayed on his sleeping form, fear at what he might say filling me.

The Reaper stepped up beside me, his hand hovering over the top of the prince's glowing form. "Your princess did what she had wished to do, but she did not think of the repercussions her action would have on her dear prince."

"Then it's true," I started, "the shadows are not truly defeated and they still lay exactly where they were when the spell was cast. Inside of the prince."

"Yes," the Reaper shook his head, a sadness coming over his face, "an unfortunate side effect. But that is where you come in."

"Me?" I held my hands up in confusion. "What can I do?"

"If you wish to leave this place you must do what I should have done years ago and destroy the shadows."

I stepped back from the prince's body, shaking my head. "Then why don't you do it now?"

"Because to destroy them you must go into his mind, and he does not know me, but you..." he pointed at me. "You have a connection with him through your lady love. He might just let you in."

"Why do you even care? If he is stuck like this and the shadows can't get out then why not just leave him like this?" I gestured a hand at the body. I didn't want the prince stuck like this, but I wasn't going to fix something that didn't need fixing.

"I care, as you ask," The Reaper turned his gaze from me to the form of the prince, and then said softly, "Because he is my son."

His son? The UnSeelie Prince was the son of the Reaper? How could that be?

There was nothing in the history books about who had sired the prince. We had never had a king, at least not in my time. Any who might have remembered a time when we had one had never brought it up either. Seer would be the only one that would be forthcoming with such information anyways.

"How is this possible?" I looked to the prince and then to the Reaper, the resemblance between the two now unmistakable.

"Let me tell you a story about a man and the choice between two queens."

CHAPTER

KAT

AS A HUMAN, I had never been in the UnSeelie Palace. Sure I had been in the garden a few times but never the palace itself.

Unlike the Seelie Queen, the UnSeelie Queen didn't force the decor to be solely focused on white and gold. The palace was covered in an array of colors. Dark purples to bright red. So much so that it almost clashed with each other but somehow it worked.

I made my way up the palace steps and into the main entryway. There, a palace guard started to stop me but took one look at me and quickly changed his guarded stance to a low bow.

"Your highness, we were not expecting you. If you had let us know you were coming we'd have prepared a proper greeting befitting of your station," the guard with copper hair, and a sprinkle of freckles across the bridge of his nose stuttered out, making his pointed ears twitch.

"This isn't an official visit. So don't worry about it." I waved him off walking by him while taking in what had changed since I had last been there.

When I was fully Fae and engaged to Dorian I had visited the palace with him a few times. Mostly for looks rather than actually wanting to be here. We had spent most of our time in his bedroom rather than walking around the palace itself.

The entryway, though, was as I remembered. Large and open, there were glass murals depicting scenes that I had never found out the meaning behind. One of a woman crying by a pool of water that reflected a dark face. Another much like the statue in the garden showing two women, a man, and a tree. Stories that had probably been long before my time and would require another trip to the library to find the answers. Something that wasn't on my to-do list anytime soon.

"Katherine." My attention was pulled from the decor at the sound of Mab's voice. She stood at the top of a grand staircase, her black dress glittering around her as it cascaded along the stairs.

"Sorry to come by unannounced, but I'm here about—"

"Finally," she cut me off with an impatient smile. "I see you have finally realized what I have been saying all along."

"Yes," I started again; a bit perturbed that she cut me off. "I got a message from Chess. He's in the shadow realm, I saw him briefly through a mirror, but I couldn't get through to him for more than a few seconds."

"Of course not," she scoffed as if what I had said was a known fact. "If the Shadow Realm was so easily accessible everyone would be wanting to visit their loved ones who were banished there." She gestured with a hand for me to follow her as she moved away from the stairs and down the corridor.

Taking the stairs two at a time, I hurried to catch up with her, my breathing heavy by the time I reached her. "The only way I know into the Shadow Realm is through the door in the Between but since the handle is gone and my magic is currently mad at me, I'm at a loss on how to get to them."

"The handle is gone because I took it."

Stopping mid-step, my mouth dropped. "What? You took it? I thought it was my mother to try and hide her dirty work with the shadows."

Mab gave a half laugh before turning to me. "Everything does not revolve around Tatiana, no matter how much she might think otherwise. I took the door handle long before the shadows became a problem. Long before you were born."

"So, do you know another way in?"

She gave me a look that was so Dorian that I couldn't help but smile. Returning my grin with one of her own, she led me through the hallways of the UnSeelie Palace. A sense of nostalgia came over me as we walked down the corridor. The last time I had been here had been with Dorian.

He had broken me out of the Seelie Palace a few months after we had become engaged. Even though I had agreed to the marriage, my mother had still sought to keep me under lock and key. Dorian didn't understand that, and really neither had I. I still didn't, to be honest.

Dorian had snuck me out one night. Leading me by the hand, laughing and stopping to kiss me every once in a while, we had run down these halls without a care in the world. Now standing in the very hallway where we had spent so much time, where we had been so in love, I felt guilty.

"So, many memories in these halls," Mab commented glancing over her shoulder with a knowing smile and then frowned, "they have been too quiet the last century."

I wrapped my arms around my midsection, her words making my guilt even worse. Not only had I dumped her son, which caused his spiral that ended in him being in the Shadow Realm, but I had also been the reason she had been alone all this time. The curse my mother had placed on Dorian hadn't just punished him but also punished his mother. It seemed I had a lot to make up for, starting with getting Chess and Dorian out of the Shadow Realm.

Mab walked down the hallway, her steps echoing in the silence we had fallen into. I wondered where we were headed until she started up a winding staircase and then I didn't have to wonder anymore. The door we ended at was that of Mab's own bedroom.

I'd never been in the room myself. The one time I had tried to enter Dorian had warned me away. Something about her liking her privacy or what not. Now I wasn't so sure. I think she just wanted to keep him out.

I waited for Mab to open the door, but she stopped before it with a sweep of her skirts. She folded her hands over each other and leveled her gaze on me.

"What are you waiting for? The longer we stand here and talk the longer God knows what is happening to Chess and your son."

She waved me off as if my words had no consequence. "They have been there for half a year now, they aren't going anywhere. Besides," she gave me a secret smile, "I have it on good authority that they are perfectly fine and waiting for your arrival."

"Then what are we waiting for? Let's go." I tried to push past her, but she stopped me with her hand.

"Before I show you the way, I have to know." The way she paused reminded me of those soap operas where the main character was just about to reveal that they weren't who they say they were but their evil twin. It didn't ease the anxiety I had to get Chess and Dorian out, which I suppose was the point.

"What is it?"

"Are you willing to do whatever it takes to get them back? If not then I will not even waste my time leading you into my private domain." She pressed her hand on the door of her bedroom as if it were a sacred place.

My brows furrowed, and I quickly said, "Yes, of course. That's not even a question."

"Good, then let us proceed." Mab turned the knob to her bedroom and opened the door.

As it swung open, my heart lifted in my chest and then sank like a stone. What the hell? I was expecting something like a dominatrix lair or maybe even for her to have a secret obsession with pink frills. Sadly, neither was true. The room was completely ordinary.

She had a four poster bed with dark blue covers. The nightstands on either side of the bed matched the standing wardrobe. The only thing that was out of place from a usual bedroom was a large mirror that took up most of one wall.

Moving into the room, I started for the mirror. One thing I knew about the Underground, everything had to do with mirrors. For the mirror to be here for no other reason than for her to stare at herself all day would be too hard to believe. If she was anything like my mother, the mirror contained something that couldn't be left open to the masses.

"You are a quick one, I give you that." Mab approached me from behind as I stood before the mirror, her reflection showing with mine. "But then again, your human side has always been the more resourceful one."

Ignoring her insult to my prior self, I stared into the mirror trying to find some kind of difference. There was no frame on the mirror, so I couldn't activate it like all the rest. If it was the entrance to the Shadow Realm, how did I get inside?

"As you can tell," she traced her fingertips along the surface of the mirror causing it to ripple beneath her touch. "This mirror is not like the rest."

"Will it get me into the Shadow Realm?"

149

"Yes, it's actually the only way in and out left. Even my cousin does not know about this mirror." Her voice became low and filled with remorse. "It has been my best-kept secret for so long it is hard to share it with anyone. Even to get my precious son back."

"But why even have it if it is so dangerous?" I gestured a hand at the mirror. "Isn't the Shadow Realm the reason we are in this mess in the first place? I would think that all the portals to it would have been destroyed."

"They were, except for this one." A flash of guilt crossed her face and then it dawned on me.

"You're the reason they got out, aren't you?" I pointed an accusatory finger at her. When she winced and didn't deny it, anger filled me, my magic coming to the surface fully recharged and ready to play. "This is all your fault."

"Now, now, let's not be too hasty." She waved her hands at me as if it would deflect me from unleashing my rage on her.

Everything that had happened to me from Alice's trick, to my death, to all those who had died since then, had been because of her and this damn mirror. She was lucky I didn't turn her in on the spot.

"I just have one question." I held a finger up to her and held back a smile, as she visibly relaxed. At least I knew that even she was scared of me. "What was so important that you would put everyone at risk by keeping this mirror?"

"The very same reason you are willing to go in to save your Cheshire." Her eyes became misty with emotion. "Love."

"So, what? Your guy got exiled to the Shadow Realm and because you couldn't let go and move on, you put everyone in danger?" I understood going to extremes for your loved ones but this was ridiculous. Though, in her place, I couldn't say I wouldn't do the same. I still felt the ache in my chest where Chess should be. If given the chance to ease that pain, I might be tempted to break a rule or two.

"Let's just say I fell for the wrong prince." She gave a grim smile and then turned back to the mirror. "I am sorry for what happened. That is why I accepted my cousin's punishment without argument. Now, I wish to make up for my crimes against my son," she pressed her hand to her mouth with a sob, "he did not deserve any of this, and I fear that his torment is far from over."

"What do you mean?" I cocked my head to the side. "What's so horrible about the Shadow Realm? Isn't it just like dark and barren? I mean, that's what I saw when I talked to Chess."

Shaking her head, she placed her hand on the mirror. "There are more dangers in the Shadow Realm than just the shadows themselves. Those who were exiled there still reside in its arms."

"Okay, so it's a realm full of convicts. Good to know." I nodded my head and started to place my hand on the mirror as well but she grabbed it in a tight grip.

"No, they are not simply convicts. While some of those that were sent there did not deserve to be there but were on the wrong side of your mother's temper, there are others who must be kept there at all costs. They are dangerous not just to others but also to themselves. You must heed caution before stepping into the Shadow Realm."

"So, stay away from the convicts and watch out for the big bad. Got it. Anything else?"

"You are not taking this seriously, Katherine." The way she said my name reminded me of my human mother when she was trying to lecture me on decorum. "You are not simply going to be able to walk in there and walk out with our men like it's a regular Sunday walk."

"I know that," I huffed, "There are dangers untold around every corner. Isn't that the way it's been since I stepped foot back in the Underground? Believe me, I took on the shadows. I'm sure I'll be fine."

"But are you ready to take on the Reaper?" Mab's questioned, the mention of the Reaper finally getting my attention.

"The Reaper?"

"Yes," she nodded, "it won't just be the residents that you will have to watch out for but the Reaper himself. You are going into his domain and he does not take kindly to visitors. Believe me, I know." That sadness in her eyes came back again.

"I see what you mean."

"So, are you, Katherine Nottington, willing to take the chance, that by saving them, you, yourself, may not come back out again?" she shook her head in warning,

153

"And trust me when I say, nobody here would dare try to get you out."

CHAPTER

CHESS

"I WASN'T ALWAYS the Reaper," Eugene started, turning away from the prince's form to move off to the side into a darkened area not reached by the torchlight. "The Reaper is not someone who is born into the power. It is passed down from generation to generation and when my time came I did not want to go."

As he approached the statue, a light flared to life in a bowl next to him. The statue came to life under the glow of the light and what I saw made me gasp. The statue had the exact likeness of the UnSeelie Queen herself. She blinked down at the Reaper and smiled. The smile had so much love and devotion in it that I had a sneaky suspicion that I knew the story he was to tell.

"Do you know how the shadows came to be?" the Reaper asked me, not turning away from the statue of the queen.

"I only know that they were Fae cast out from our world. When they were sent here is when they conformed into the evil thing they are now." I peeked over at the prince from the corner of my eye as if speaking about them might make him wake.

"I suppose it is best to start at the beginning then so you can understand better."

"I would appreciate that." I nodded my head in consensus. The whole picture would be delightful, especially since up until this point Kat and I had only ever gotten bits and pieces of the original story. Knowing the whole of it would make it easier to defeat the shadows once and for all.

"There was once a time when the Fae outnumbered the humans, and as you know, we Fae survive on the dreams of humans, thus making our long-term livability depressing at best. So, the queens came together with their best advisers to figure out how to increase the human population."

"Many of them wanted to send some of our Fae out into the human world to breed with the humans," the Reaper paused in his story to give me a lopsided grin, "back then we were quitc fertile and could easily fix the imbalance between our two species."

"But," I interjected, "that doesn't make sense. Why would we go mate with humans that would just make more half-bloods, and Fae cannot feed on the dreams of other Fae for very long? So, they would just be making more humans we couldn't feed on."

"Ah, but half-bloods dreams are different than a full-blooded Faes dreams. The thing that set the Fae apart from the humans is our inability to work out our issues inside of our minds. It is probably why so many Fae end up being petty and selfish." He shrugged like it wasn't really important. "But the majority of half-bloods would inherit the human ability to dream full vivid dreams that are full of wonder and imagination. Things we Fae could never hope to create on our own." I opened my mouth to point out once more that the dreams of half-bloods were poor substitutes for human dreams, but he cut me off, "Now they were aware this was not a permanent solution. That it would take years for those half-bloods to breed with other humans and thus so on and so forth." He waved his hand in front of him in a continuous cycle.

"Eventually, the humans would catch up to us in the long run, thus ensuring the survival of our species. The whole of the group was in agreement that this was the best of plans except for one." The Reaper's face clouded over with a kind of hatred I had never seen on another Fae's face. "Moradoc."

"Who?"

"Of course, you would never have heard of him, since his name has long been erased from our history. An attempt to hide the evil that came from him. Not that it helped." His hand reached up to stroke the face of the queen's before he dropped it to his side and turned to me.

"Moradoc believed that mating with the humans was an abomination. That we would sully our line, our magic, by daring to fraternize with what we saw as food. He proposed that we gather the humans up like cattle and force them to procreate so that we may have enough food to go around, as well as the benefit of feeding straight from the source. We all know what can happen when we do that," he leveled his gaze on me.

Feeding on human dreams from a distance was easy enough and gave plenty of power to any normal Fae. There were some Fae though who only wished to feed directly from the source and that could become a problem. Taking power from the dreams of humans can be tricky and hard to control. It takes a great deal of power to make sure that we only take what we need without killing the human in the process. Otherwise, the human population would drop and then eventually we would cease to exist. So, doing what this Moradoc guy wanted to do was a huge no-no. Fae have been cast out for less.

"So, as you can imagine they shot down his idea, and that didn't make him very happy. He deserted his place as an adviser, and they thought they had heard the last of him. The queens' moved forward with their plan to increase the human populace and for a while, it worked. The human race began to triple in size and became such an overwhelming number that we were no longer in risk of ever running out of food."

"But while the queens' celebrated their victory in saving their people, Moradoc was waiting. Biding his time until he could get what he wanted. Moradoc did not simply want to enslave the human race to save our people; he wanted power. He did not want to stay a lowly adviser; he wanted to take over all of the Underground. Combining both sides so that he was the supreme ruler. To do that, though, he needed power. Power, in which, he would not find in the Fae realm."

"He rallied his supporters and tried to sneak into the human world to take the power he needed to succeed. This was before we had the nice reception area we have now, back then we were able to simply go in and out of our world and into theirs without a Between to stop in. That was created later. The queens' only learned of his plan as he was making his way into the human world."

"With Moradoc in captivity, they debated for days and weeks about what to do with him and his supporters. The UnSeelie Queen wished to kill them all, but her cousin, the Seelie Queen, did not want to shed any Fae blood. The Seelie Queen struck a deal with my father, the previous Reaper."

"He would take Moradoc into the Shadow Realm and keep him there in exchange for one of them to provide an heir for his son, me." His lips twisted at his explanation. "You can imagine I wasn't too thrilled to be traded off but when I met the queens' everything changed."

"How did you end up with the UnSeelie Queen? I mean, not that I'm complaining, I've met the Seelie Queen and of the two I would have chosen the same." The White Queen as Kat liked to call her was a heartless bitch that had put her own daughter up to be sacrificed to fix her mistakes. If I had the choice between two crazy queens, I would most definitely choose mine.

"There wasn't really a choice to me. While Tatiana was beautiful and definitely interested, she was already promised to another, and I wasn't about to get in the middle of a prior arrangement, even just for one night of pleasure. But Mab." The sigh he released showed so much longing in it that it made my own heart ache for Kat.

"She was everything to me the moment we met. She's the reason I didn't want to become the Reaper when my father's time was done. I spent several glorious years with her, in which, we conceived our child." His dark blue eyes turned to where the prince lay. "When the time came for me to leave and take my father's place, I didn't want to go. I wanted to stay and raise our child and be with the woman I had fallen for even through our strange meeting."

"I was prepared to tell my father no, that I would live my own life, and he would just have to find someone else. As you can imagine, he did not take my decision happily. With Moradoc in our realm, he needed me more than ever. If Moradoc wasn't such a threat then maybe I could spend more time with my family but that wasn't the case." His eyes narrowed, his lips becoming a tight line on his face. "Not to be put down by my father's words, I came up with a plan. I snuck into his storeroom where I knew there was something that would help me change my fate. You've heard of the tree of life, correct?"

I nodded. Kat had told me of the tree that had called her back to the Underground, but I'd not seen it for myself. The tree that had also helped her die and come back to herself. The same tree that was now nonexistent.

"Well, the original tree had long since perished and left behind a few seeds in case there was a great time of need." He shrugged. "I was young and naive and thought my need was great enough that it justified using those seeds."

"I stole my father's seeds and snuck into the UnSeelie Realm where I was to meet up with Mab. She showed me a grove in the Orchard that we could plant them so that nobody would find out what we had done." He laughed bitterly running a hand over his face. "I was such a fool then, thinking my actions wouldn't have consequences. That I was helping not just myself, but everyone in the Underground."

"Mab, bless her, has an affinity for plant life, much like your princess. She was able to cultivate the seed, forcing it to grow to

163

full height without having to wait the millennia it would have taken."

I cut him off, my mind catching up to where the story would surely end. "You used the fruit, didn't you?"

The guilty expression that passed over his face was all the answer I needed. From what I had heard nothing good ever came from wishing on the fruit from that tree. It never gave you exactly what you wished for, it's interpretation much different than what you intended to happen.

"I wished that Moradoc and his followers would disappear. That I might finally be free to live my life as I chose. The tree granted my wish." He crossed his arms over his chest, his eyes downcast. "I came home to my father to see if it had worked only to find out Moradoc had vanished into thin air. My father was beside himself and had no idea what happened. That is when I pleaded for him to give me more time with Mab, and with no other reason to make me stay he granted it."

"But it wouldn't last. Not long after I had returned to Mab's side did a messenger come to me of my father's demise. My wish did indeed get rid of Moradoc, but it had made him and his followers something intangible, allowing Moradoc to somehow figure out how to harness the power of the Shadow Realm. He took the darkness meant to keep the dead from straying into himself and with it his followers. They became what you now know as the shadows."

"Not, living or dead, they can feed on the Shadow Realms energy as if they were feeding on human dreams. Sending them back here was one of the worst things your princess could have done. Thus, why I had to put my son to sleep. With him in solid form, the shadows are easier to contain and keep from devouring all of the Shadow Realm and its power. But I can't hold him forever. Eventually, he will overpower my spell and then seek vengeance once more."

"That is why I ask you to save him." The Reaper said finishing his story. "You are my only hope to get my son back and to right the wrong I had so selfishly created from making that wish."

His story made my mind whirl. There was so much information that I had never believed could be true. Everyone, including myself, believed the Shadows were created because of the Seelie Queen sending them to the Shadow Realm, but it hadn't been that at all.

While Tatiana had indeed done some deplorable things, she was only trying to clean up the mess that was made by someone else. Meaning she wasn't as cold and heartless as everyone thought her to be. That Kat thought her to be. Kat had based her entire relationship with her mother on this one thing alone, and she needed to be set straight but first, there was more to do.

"Say I do decide to help you, how would I even get into his mind? And how would I get out again?"

"Leave that up to me. I will help you get inside my son's mind, but once you are in I'm afraid," he paused and shook his head, "I won't be able to help you get out again. If you clear Dorian of the Shadows then he will wake up and you will come out on your own but if you don't..."

"I'll be stuck there," I finished for him. I'd heard stories similar to this and it was easy to guess the outcome. I stared down at the prince's form, my face scrunched in concentration. What was I going to do?

CHAPTER

KAT

GOING INTO THE Shadow Realm would mean I would be alone. Which normally wasn't a problem. In the past, I had never had an issue being alone. I actually thrived on it.

Even in college, I hadn't been one to go out and party. I preferred to sit in my room and read. It wasn't because people didn't try to be my friend. More like I had a low tolerance for bullshit, and the longer I was friends with someone, the more drama came with it. So I had come to the conclusion that being alone was better. At least, at the time.

Now, I hardly got a moment to myself. There was always one crisis after another. One Fae or another that needed my help. And with Alice living with me, she was always bringing Hatter or some other poor Fae home. It made it hard to keep to myself.

I suppose I could have hidden in my bedroom until they had all gone, but then I'd be in there all the time and god damn it, it was my house. Well, technically my grandmother's house but by relation that meant it was mine.

So, if I was so good with being alone why was the idea of going to the shadow realm by myself so worrying? Was it because it was unknown territory? I could go to the Seelie court alone because I had been there before with others. But the Shadow Realm? That was a whole other ball game.

I could ask Mop or even Trip to come with me. I knew they would drop everything to help me. But I also knew this was my mistake that needed to be fixed. I couldn't drag them into it.

Alice would probably offer to come with me if I told her where I was going, but I knew I couldn't let her. She had Hatter and the other Fae that needed her help. Besides, someone had to stay behind in case something went wrong. I could end up stuck there forever and then where would the Fae be? No, Alice needed to be there so the government didn't try to force the Fae into camps or the stupid registration law they were trying to pass.

Being on my own wasn't all that bad. It meant I got to make all the decisions. Which was also a negative in a way, because now I didn't have anyone else to lean on. It was all up to me.

Yippee.

I could have delayed going. It wasn't like he was going anywhere, but I wanted Chess back, and if there was a chance that Dorian could be saved I had to try. I had no idea what awaited me on the other side or if I would just be dropping into a black pit of nothing. The Shadow Realm was supposedly where the Reaper lived. Which meant that it was kind of like the other side. Or it could be heaven. Or hell. With my track record it was more likely to be the latter.

Not letting myself stall any longer, I took a deep breath and got ready to step through the mirror only to be stopped by an annoying buzzing in my pocket. Confused for a moment at the feeling, I realized it was my phone and pulled the some how miraculously not dead device into my hand.

It was Alice. Wonderful. I hadn't let her or anyone else know what had happened with Chess and the mirror or that I was going to the Shadow Realm. I could just imagine how much she was probably freaking out since I never came home this morning.

Taking a deep breath, I pressed the button to accept the call, "Hi, Alice, how's it going? Did you and Hatter have fun last night?" I decided to start with talking about her in hopes that she wouldn't ask where I was. If I got her uncomfortable enough maybe she would hang up and leave me alone for the rest of the day. I had worlds to adventure to and people to save god damn it.

"Don't give me that," she snarled over the phone, clearly on to my ploy. "Where the hell are you?" Yelling and things smashing could be heard in the background where she was.

"I'm exactly where you left me, at Chess' of course." The beauty of cell phones was she couldn't tell if I was lying or not unless I some how lost my ability to cover the lie in my voice. Which, to be honest, wasn't likely.

"No, you are not, you big fat fibber," she snapped, her voice becoming haughty.

I crossed my arms over my chest and ignored the curious look Mab was giving me. "I am not. I'm standing right in Chess' living room right now. The purple and pink explosion is making me want to have an aneurysm just so I don't have to look at it anymore."

"No, you aren't. You know how I know that?" she paused waiting for me to deny it once more, but I held my tongue. "Because I was just there and you were no where to be found."

"Then we must of just missed each other," I chimed in, still holding on to the hope of keeping her out of this.

There was silence from her for a moment, though there was still a ruckus going on in the background that I was sure I needed to ask about at some point once I got out of my own sticky situation. After a moment or so, she let out an aggravated sigh, "Fine play it your way. If you are there then you can easily get home now. We have a situation."

Frowning, my brows crinkled together. "What do you mean a situation?"

"Hey! Stop that, leave those alone!" Alice shouted out of nowhere, confusing the hell out of me. "Sorry, that wasn't meant for you."

"It sounds like there is some kind of party going on over there. Did things go better than you planned last night with Hatter? Or am I missing something?"

She let out a short laugh. "Ha! My romantic night was cut short when we had some unexpected visitors."

"Oh really? I'm sorry to hear that, I know how much you were looking forward to getting it on with your lovey," I teased her, though my apology was sincere. Getting private time lately was hard to come by, so when we had a chance to get it, we grabbed it by the balls and didn't let it go for anyone or anything.

"Well," she huffed, "that's over and done with. The important thing is for you to get home. The president announced their plans for that Fae registration on the news today and everyone has lost their marbles," she paused and yelled at someone in the background once more before coming back on the line. "I woke up to trolls on the lawn and Faeries in the kitchen. You won't believe the mess those little critters can make."

Oh, I believed it. Faeries were one irritating creature. I wished they had some kind of magical bug spray to get rid of them. If left unchecked they would destroy my grandmother's house before I could even get there to help out. Not that I was going to, but Alice didn't know that, yet.

"I don't see what the problem is," I shrugged, though she couldn't see it, "You are better at calming the masses down than I am. I always stick my foot in my mouth and make it worse."

"But they need to see you to feel more secure. Even just being here will help the situation immensely. There are already news crews lining up outside your house, waiting to get a statement from the famed Seelie Princess."

I swallowed hard. News reporters? Yikes. Not even on my best day did I want to be subjected to the horror that was the daily news. If I was bad at talking to people, I knew there was no way I wouldn't be able to make the situation worse by talking to those vultures. Every word I had ever said to them had been twisted into some crazy fairy tale with a gruesome ending.

Taking a deep breath, I let it out and ripped the proverbial band aide off. "I'm sorry to tell you this, Alice, but you are on your own."

"What? You're not coming? I need you for this. I'm not the princess, or the moderator, I'm not anything. I can't handle a problem this big." She kept rambling on and then when she finally took a breath I jumped in.

"I'm not at Chess'."

"I knew it!" she screeched, causing me to wince and pull the phone from my ear. "You big fat liar face. I knew you weren't at Chess'. Just missed you my fanny."

"Yes, yes. You were right," I grumbled.

"If you aren't at Chess' where are you and how long will it take you to get here?"

"About that..." I started and scratched the back of my head as I gave a nervous laugh. "I'm in the UnSeelie Palace about two seconds away from going to the Shadow Realm."

There was a long pause that had me looking at the phone to make sure I hadn't lost the call or my phone hadn't finally died.

Nope she was still there. I hoped she hadn't died of shock, or worse, the Faeries had gotten to her.

Just thinking of all the horrible scenarios that could have gone down had me calling into the phone, "Alice? Are you there? Blink once for yes and two for no. Wait, no. Don't do that cause I can't see you. Just say something damn it!"

"I'm here." Was her low reply. Those two words held so much contained rage that I was half tempted to pretend I lost the call on my side.

"Oh, good," I gave a nervous laugh once more, "I thought I'd lost you for a second. But anyways like I said, I'm about to head out and can't help you."

"Katherine Nottington, don't you dare hang up on me!" the tone of her voice had my finger pausing on the end button and then the stupid person in me actually listened and didn't hang up.

"What?"

"What do you mean what?" she shrilled, "You were just going to go to some dangerous realm without mentioning it to anyone? What if you die? What if you got stuck there forever and then who would take your place? The Fae community is already rocky at best, and if the one person they look up to gets herself killed, then who would be here to fight for them?"

"One, chill the fuck out," I started, an irritated tick starting at my eyebrow at her words. "Two, I didn't not tell anyone, the queen knows I'm here, it's her portal, duh."

"Well, that's just lovely."

"Hey, can the sarcasm, I'm not done yet," I interrupted her before she could go into an even longer tangent. "I'm not leaving the Fae completely defenseless. That's what you are for," She tried to interrupt me but I kept talking, "now before you try to tell me you aren't the one for the job, you are wrong. Who has gone out of their way to find all the Fae in our area? Who's the one who made sure that they had places to live? Or work? It wasn't me."

"But that's beside the point, you had just lost the love of your life, you had a reason to be neglectful."

"Bullshit. I was too wrapped up in my own problems to care about anything else going on around me. Hell, if you didn't live with me I wouldn't have any idea what was going on with the Fae in the human world to begin with. If they trust anyone to help them through this time, it's you."

"If you say so," she replied with uncertainty.

"I know so," I assured her and then turned to Mab who wasn't even pretending not to listen to our conversation. "In fact, I'm going to send the queen to help you out. It would do the humans some good to see an authority figure besides me working for the Faes benefit."

My words caused Mab to raise a brow at me, but she didn't comment otherwise. Smart woman.

"All right, if you say so, but this place needs cleaned up if we are having royalty visit. Your laundry has been strewn everywhere."

I groaned, those little Faerie bastards better not have messed up my room. I wasn't a particularly organized person but the system I had worked for me. If they screwed it up I wouldn't find anything for weeks.

After I said my goodbyes and hung up the phone, I turned to Mab. "Well, you heard what is going on. You wanted to be there for your people. Now you will get your chance.

The humans are going through with the plan to force us to register."

At my words, Mab's face hardened. Her eyes filled with a determination and even I wouldn't want to stand in her way.

"We shall see about that," was all she said before she swept out of the room, her dress fluttering behind her, leaving me utterly alone with the mirror.

With Mab well on her way, I shook off my nerves and took another deep breath before letting it out. Placing one foot in front of the other, my eyes straight ahead, I stepped through the mirror.

CHAPTER

CHESS

I WISH I could say that when I saw Dorian's sleeping form that I was ecstatic that he had survived, but I'm not that good of a person. The only thing I felt was annoyance and anger.

This man, this petty, spiteful man had done everything in his power to destroy what Kat and I had. Even before he had joined the Shadows he hadn't acted for one minute like the dutiful ruler he had once been.

Before the whole thing with Kat, I didn't see the prince often. He was too busy messing with the lower Fae to bother with the moderator. The majority of the time he avoided me.

It had been just after the Seelie Queen had shoved the twins onto me. Not long before Kat showed up in the Underground. I didn't know if it was a sign of things changing or not, but thinking back to it now, I wanted to think it was the Undergrounds way of warning us. Not that we listened.

I'd been hanging out at the base of my willow as usual, completely bored out of my mind when I heard an owl hoot. Anyone who had a lick of sense in the UnSeelie Court knew that an owl only meant one thing. The dark prince.

Cursed as he was at the time, it wasn't smart to mess with him. He was unstable and unpredictable. One never knew what kind of mood he would be in. Just the week before he had killed two changelings because they had annoyed him. There was no telling what would set him off.

Now that I knew the Seelie Queen had cursed him, I think it was her way of punishing not just the prince, but also all of the UnSeelie for daring to take her daughter from her, not that the rest of us had anything to do with it. Though, the rest had welcomed Alice with open arms and by association, I supposed that made us all guilty in her eyes.

The owl hoot was followed by a flutter of wings and then the vines that hung around the willow parted to reveal the prince in all his broodiness. His bright blue eyes darted around the area, a scowl on his lips before they landed on me. They curled up into a playful sort of cruel grin that said he wasn't here for anything I would enjoy.

Standing to my feet, I tapped my riding crop against my thigh, the stinging pain of it keeping my own temper in check as I greeted him, "Your highness, what do I have the honor?"

"Half-breed, I'd always wondered why you are here. What makes you so special to give you the role of moderator?" he cocked his head to the side as if in thought. I didn't answer him knowing anything I said would just set him off. It was a fine line we walked with the dark prince. One I didn't plan to fall off any time soon.

"Are you just the queen's lackey or her lover as well? Are you so good at what you do that she would reward you with a pretend position?" the mocking in his voice caused me to clack the crop harder against my thigh.

"My position is hardly pretend." I couldn't help but answer, regretting it instantly when his eyes sharpened on me.

"Really? Is that what she tells you? Because the way I see it is you are nothing more than a flunky with a pretty face. Made for their entertainment and nothing more. Not someone like me, with real power." The prince's face contorted into a pained expression, the symbols on his face lighting up and then going out.

I wished I'd known that day what that light meant. That it meant he was fighting against his curse. Then I wouldn't have done what I had done next, but alas, it wasn't so.

Before the prince could spout another insult, I had twisted in place and appeared behind him. Shoving him with a booted foot, I knocked him to the ground.

"Who is bowing to who now, your highness?" I mocked, laughing at his prone form.

The prince growled and my laughter was cut off mid laugh as an invisible hand wrapped around my throat. I struggled against his hold on me unable to breathe. My hands scratched at an unseen force.

"Do not forget your place, half-breed. You may have been given position of moderator but you do not dictate me," he hissed in my face before the force holding me up disappeared, dropping me to the ground. Heaving in deep breaths, I glared up at the prince who lorded his power over me.

The memory caused me to have quite a conundrum on my hand. On the one side, I could let Dorian die and with him the Shadows. It would ensure that the Shadows were truly gone and that they wouldn't come back. It was a logical choice. It should have been the easy choice. Dorian would die and the Shadows would be gone and any drama and chance of him coming between Kat and me would be eliminated.

On the other hand, I could go into his mind and risk everything to save him. Or, I could get rid of the Shadows and Dorian would be safe, but I also ran the risk of getting stuck in his mind myself.

I felt like I had a little devil on my shoulder whispering to me. "But no one would know if I let him die. Not Kat, not anyone back home."

It was tempting to just listen to that voice. He had caused me nothing but pain and heartache as well as put Kat in a horrible position. Sadly though, if I let him die, I highly doubted that the Reaper would help me get back home. In fact, I was positive he wouldn't.

There was also the fact that if Kat did find out, she would be devastated. Though, she might say she didn't care about Dorian anymore, there was still a piece of her that still loved him and would always love him. It hurt for me to admit it but it was true. Which was all the more reason that I should let him rot.

Turning to face the Reaper, I sighed. "What do I need to do?" Even as I asked the question I regretted my decision. I had a sneaky feeling that this would somehow come back to bite me in the ass.

The Reaper didn't seem to notice the lack of enthusiasm in my voice. Which was good considering if he thought for one second I was going to let his son die, he might make sure I never saw Kat again. Even worse, he could stick me in some kind of hellhole made for the really bad Fae. I was sure there had to be some kind of place for them.

"I don't decide that actually," The Reapers voice cut through my thoughts. My eyes jerked up to his face where he had an amused look in his eyes. Had he been able to hear me this whole time? I had forgotten he was able to do that. Damn.

Chuckling at my distress, the Reaper shook his head. "No, I don't listen in all the time. You were just projecting your thoughts so loudly it was easy to pick up on what you were thinking. Don't worry everyone thinks that the first time they meet me."

Frowning in confusion, I stared up at him. "So, you don't decide who goes where?"

"I only bring the souls here. Once here they move on on their own. To heaven? To hell? Who knows?" He shrugged. "I'm not dead."

"You're not?" I looked him up and down trying to discern exactly what he was. I had thought he was something more than Fae but his previous story made it out that he was just like the rest of us.

"No. I'm not." His gaze settled firmly on my face. "The thing you must understand is

185

that I am the same as any other Fae. I just happen to have the ability to cater to the dead."

"Then what about those glowing things you said were spirits. How come they are still here?" I waved a hand toward the outside where I had first seen them.

"Those are the ones who will not be put to rest. They refuse to go beyond to the final resting place. Thus, they linger here trying to take anyone they can with them into their misery."

"So then what happens when you die? Does someone take your place?"

"Of course I will. I'm not immortal," he scoffed and moved over to where Dorian's body lay. "And as for who will take my place, that highly depends on if you will save my son. Like my father and I, he will be trained to cater to the souls of the deceased until he has a child that will take his place. Allowing him to retire and do whatever he likes with his life."

From the Reaper's previous story I had a feeling I knew what he wanted to do with the remainder of his life. The UnSeelie Queen had never married nor had she ever shown the slightest interest in having a king. It wouldn't be surprising to know she had been waiting for him all this time.

Clapping my hands together, I rubbed them for good measure before moving next to the Reaper. I cast my eyes on the prince and asked, "So, what do I have to do? How do I get inside of his mind?"

"It's quite simple really. Place your hand here." He grasped my hand nearest to him and led it over to hover above the prince's chest. He tried to lower it down so that I was touching him but I resisted.

"You have nothing to be afraid of, he won't wake up just from you touching him," he chuckled at my reluctance, "This isn't even the hard part."

"It isn't?" His words weren't reassuring at all. I was regretting agreeing to this more and more and it hadn't even begun.

"No, the hard part will be getting you out. This part will only take you letting me into your mind as long as you don't shut me out, then you will easily be able to slip into my son's head. Once there it will be up to you to figure out how to dispel the shadows."

Frowning hard at him, I hopefully replied, "Any ideas of how to do that?"

The Reaper thought about it for a moment, his grip on my hand lessening, but he didn't remove it from where he held it above the prince's body. "There will more than likely be a series of tests. Things that the prince has to overcome to weaken the shadows. Once they are to the point where they can't latch onto his mind anymore they should be easy to kick out of his mind."

Should be? I didn't like the sound of that. Everything he was saying sounded like theory. Like he didn't know for sure if it would work and was just making it up as he went along and hoping it would work. Which was bad for me, since I was the one who was putting my tail on the line for a man I didn't even like.

"Very well, let's get this over with so I can go home," I growled, my tail whipping behind me, making me unable to hide my nervousness completely.

"Certainly, now place your hand here." He lowered my hand down, and this time I didn't resist. When my palm touched the middle of the prince's chest I held my breath expecting some kind of reaction from his body or to get some sort of shock, but nothing happened. I guess the Reaper was right on that account. He was truly gone from this world.

"Now," the Reaper continued, "close your eyes. It will help you to visualize what I am saying." Pursing my lips in displeasure, I did what he asked. My anxiety shot through the roof each moment I couldn't see.

"Good. Now, I want you to picture a door. It doesn't matter what it looks like, it's the functionality that matters," he answered my unasked question before I could even formulate it in my mind.

A solid rectangular door with dark oak finish formulated in my mind. Why this particular door? I wasn't sure. It just seemed right as it came into my mind's eye.

"I want you to reach for the door handle." His words echoed not in my ears but in my mind as my hand reached for the brass handle. In my mind, the handle was cool to the touch as if it hadn't been used in a while. If I were to get scholarly on it, I would say that it was a representation of the prince's comatose state. His mind and body were unused and thus lacking in heat.

"This part is very important. So listen closely." I focused on his words as much as I could, not wanting to do anything that might cause me to get stuck in the prince's mind, or worse, my own.

"As you open the door, you must not close yourself off. You have to imagine you are light as air so that you may float from your consciousness to his. Understood?"

"Yes." I nodded but realized that it was inside of my head and I hadn't really physically done it. This was going to be really strange, I could already tell.

"Good. Then open the door."

My wrist twisted as I unlatched the lock and did as he said. Light, airy, I am floating through space. Nothing can weigh me down.

I thought I was doing a great job until I tried to step through the door. Then it was like an anchor fell on my chest. I couldn't breathe and all thoughts of feather-likeness shot from my mind.

"He's fighting you," the Reaper's voice rang in my mind, "He doesn't realize you are trying to help him. You have to reassure him so he will let you in."

Reassure him? The guy who hated my guts as much as I did his? That was easier said than done.

Prince? I said in my mind feeling quite silly. *It's Cheshire. I am here to help. You have to let me in or you will die.*

Nothing happened for a moment. There was no answer, no evidence that he had even heard me. Then the entrance to the door was no longer weighing me down, I was light and weightless once more. As I stepped through a sick feeling overcame me just before the door slammed shut behind me. What the hell had I gotten myself into?

CHAPTER

KAT

THE LIQUID THAT enveloped me was unlike the others. This one wasn't cold. It was glacial. It burned like fire where it touched, and it felt like it lasted forever.

Finally, I fell out of the mirror on the other side. I collapsed to the ground and took in deep heaving breaths. It took me a few moments before I realized the pain was gone. I sat up and glanced at myself, turning my hands over in confusion. There were no burns, no markings where there should have been.

Mab had said the Shadow Realm was not for the living, but the dead. Those who were sent here still alive wouldn't be welcomed at any point. Perhaps this was what she meant when she warned me before I stepped through the glass. Maybe that was its way of trying to get me to turn back?

I had expected a lot of things when I came through the mirror, but what I didn't expect was it to be so blah. Darkness stretched as far as I could see and the fog was thick enough to make soup out of it. And what was up with the fucking mirrors? They were everywhere. Did someone rob a mirror store? Or were they just really bad at decorating?

I moved around the area, the dirt ground beneath my feet making the area even more depressing. If this was the afterlife I wasn't looking forward to it. If the dreary atmosphere wasn't enough, the utter lack of anyone else would have sealed the deal.

I was all for alone time but this was ridiculous.

I started toward the mirror area, my eyes flickering from one mirror to the next. Each surface reflected my face. If they were used for communication like Chess had done with me in his bathroom, they weren't active now.

Kneeling on the ground next to one of the mirrors, my hand reached out to touch the frame to see if I could activate it with my magic. The instant my hand touched the metal frame, the mirror's surface changed and showed the wall on the opposite side of the mirror in my hallway at home.

I moved from the mirror to another one. Not hesitating this time, I touched the frame. This one reflected the mirror in my bathroom. The next one showed my bedroom.

I collapsed to the ground with a huff, my heart beating in my chest like a thundering drum. Had Chess been watching me this whole time? Trying to communicate but unable to get through?

My eyes burned as my throat clogged up. All this time I had been thinking he was gone, that I had to move on, and he had been right here the entire time.

"So, you must be the long lost Seelie Princess." Glancing up from where I had fallen to pieces, my eyes widened at the woman before me.

She was clad in a crimson gown, the neckline plunging so low I could see her navel. If I had worn it I'd have tripped and fallen out of it with the first step, but the way she moved in it was like it was part of her. Where she moved it moved, slithering along the dirt ground like a snake.

"Who are you?" my voice came out scratchy and I hated it. I had a feeling that any weakness in front of her would be a very bad idea.

"Are all humans so rude? Cheshire wasn't half as rude as you. He at least introduced himself before he started demanding answers."

At the mention of Chess, I jumped to my feet, launching myself onto her, my hands clutching her shoulders. "You know where Chess is? Was he here? Where is he now?"

"So many questions and yet you still haven't answered mine." She clucked her tongue and brushed my hands away.

Dropping my hands back to my sides, I straightened my shoulders to look her squarely in her dark eyes. "Yes, I am the long lost Seelie Princess. Now, will you please tell me where Chess is?"

"I figured that much out already, what I don't know is your name. What do they call you? It can't just be princess."

"Depends on who you ask." My eyes narrowed in suspicion as I evaded her question. Why did she want to know my name? Nothing good had ever come from a Fae wanting to know my name. That usually meant they were trying to get something from me.

"Well, what does Cheshire call you?"

Not liking the attitude coming from this woman, I gave her a nasty smile. "You can call me Lady, or better yet, moderator. Since that is what I am."

The flicker of fear in her eyes made my heart pitter-patter. She tried to cover it up with a snooty scowl. "They let someone like you be the moderator? They sure have lowered their standards since I lived in the Underground."

I couldn't help myself; I did the mean girl thing. "Well, I'd say they've raised their standards if you are here. With all that going on," I gestured to her mostly exposed torso and chest, "I'm surprised you weren't cast out sooner. What were you exiled for? The inability to keep your legs closed longer than your mouth?"

Okay, so what happened next I totally deserved. I let myself get drawn in by her petty insults and only had myself to blame. So, when I found myself going from a standing position to being knocked on my ass, it wasn't entirely surprising.

As I tried to relearn to breathe, my magic came to the surface, red alert to anything that might attack me once more. Morgana stood where she had been before but her arms turned into snakes.

Dark red and black stripped; they stretched out across the area. When she realized she had missed she slowly recoiled the slithering cretins back into her, her gaze searching for where I had jumped.

Morgana? More like freaking Medusa! Just when I thought I'd seen everything, something else happened and I had to reset my whole look on things that were abnormal.

I tensed as I watched her prepare for another attack. Her arms went rigid and her eyes narrowed as she locked on to me. Just as she was about to shoot the snakes my way again, I tucked and rolled like my life depended on it. Who said school didn't teach you anything? Though, I doubted the firefighters meant for it to be used to avoid

197

attacks by crazy snake ladies, but if it worked it worked!

"Stay still, you little twit!" she growled out in aggravation. She jerked around to find me again, the snakes that were her arms hissed at me, liquid dripped from their fangs. When it hit the floor it sizzled and caused tiny holes to form.

Note to self avoid fangs.

"Why would I do that?" I called back as I dodged yet another attack, barely avoiding getting bit in the ass. "You are trying to kill me. I don't think Cheshire would be too happy if you killed his savior." It was risky trying to use Chess as my winning piece, but from what I could tell she had a lady boner for him the size of Texas. Maybe she wouldn't want to risk making him mad?

"Pfft." She made one snake hand turn back into a regular one and flipped her hair over her shoulder. "As far as he's concerned I'm doing him a favor. Who wants to go back to the Underground with someone like you waiting for him on the other side? He would be much better off with me."

Well, it was worth a try.

"Oh, yeah?" I shot back, "Why don't you put your magic where your mouth is?" I had only just gotten the question out when her arm changed back into a snake, and this time instead of coming for me, they burrowed into the ground.

If there was one movie I hated more than anything it was Tremors. The first time I had ever watched it I was nine and I had nightmares for months. I refused to stand on solid ground and would walk on all the furniture to get anywhere. It pissed my mother off to no end, and Hillary was always yelling at me to get off the furniture. This time was no different.

Seeing those things go into the ground, I high tailed it away from where she was and scrambled onto a rock that had a mirror leaning against it. While it did have me on high ground, it didn't keep me from being pretty much trapped. All I could do was keep my eyes peeled and listen for their attack. My blood pumped in my ears as I jerked my head from side to side looking for those little fuckers.

"If only dear Cheshire could see his princess now," Morgana laughed, "Trapped like a mouse with nowhere to go."

Her laughter only caused my fear to turn to anger, and the moment I stopped looking for the snakes to reply to her was when she struck. The earth crumbled as the snake shot out of the ground and into the air. Before I could make a move to get out of the way, they whipped around, wrapping their long bodies around my frame.

Damn it. How had I fallen for her trick? I was the one who was usually distracting my enemies with my snarky remarks and here I was falling for the same ploy.

The snakes bodies constricted around me making it hard to breathe. Their heads danced around my head as if they were laughing at my pain. Trying not to panic, I took in shallow breaths. I saw it once on a TV show on snake attacks.

The more the victim panicked, the deeper they breathed and each breath they took, the snake could constrict tighter. I figured that if I wasn't giving them much room to deal with it might bide me some time. Hopefully.

The pressure on my arms and the rest of my body almost reminded me of going through the hole to get to the Between. Like it was trying to fit me in a size 2 tube top. I wasn't no petite biddy, so the imagery wasn't a pretty sight.

Trying not to think about the situation I was in, I let my magic curl up inside me. It balled up into a bundle of crackling energy, pulsating and churning, just waiting for me to release it. I waited and waited. It had to be the right moment. When she thought she was winning, that was when I would strike.

Finally, she started to get bored of how long it was taking to kill me and cocked her head to the side. "Why won't you die already? You're already in the Shadow Realm, it's not like you would have far to go."

Before she got the last few words out I let that tight ball of energy go. It rushed out of me and barreled into the bodies of the snakes. They screeched with Morgana, making my ears ring.

I didn't have time to worry about it, though. I jumped from the rock and darted across the area to hide behind a large full-length mirror. Taking in deep helpings of air, I listened to see if she would attack once more.

"I'm trying to help you, Miss Moderator," she taunted after she had finished screaming, "you'll be so much happier without all the stress of being Fae royalty, besides didn't you already kill yourself once? Cheshire would be better off with someone more secure in themselves."

While she was busy spouting off how wrong I was for him, I moved around a set of mirrors until I was on her blind side. Then with a battle cry, much like my hero, Xena, Warrior Princess, I slammed into her knocking her down to the ground.

Straddling her hips, I gripped each of her wrists in my hands as hard as I could. The pressure caused the snakes to disperse and only her hands to lie in their place. She bucked and wailed as she tried to get me off of her, but I held tight. I shoved my magic into the earth around her, forcing the deadened ground to sprout forth vines that wrapped themselves around her body and limbs.

With her thoroughly subdued, I should have gotten up. I should have left her there and went to find Chess but the power was pumping through me. The need to use more magic came to the surface at an unstoppable pace.

The magic curled into the vines pulling them tighter and tighter. Whatever else she might have said was cut off by the chokehold it had on her throat. Her face started to turn blue; her eyes bulged in their sockets. A voice in my head screamed at me to stop but it was faint. Since I had come here alone there was no one here to pull me back. No one here to make me stop. It was just my power and me.

I was just about to turn her into a squashed potato when a single tear slipped out of my eye. Confused, I reached a hand up to touch it. The action was enough to cause my magic to stall.

Looking down at the glittering moisture on my finger a stark realization filled me. Horror covered my face and I jumped up from where I sat on top of her. Now that I wasn't trying to obliterate her she was taking in deep breaths, her eyes full of terror but not brave enough to move in case I struck out again.

I skittered away from her, the temptation to finish what I started too prevalent in my mind. Stumbling to my feet, I ran from her and into the thick fog that made my stomach recoil. So engulfed by my own emotions I was easily able to push the feelings aside and keep running. To where? I didn't have a fucking clue.

CHAPTER

CHESS

I IMAGINED THE inside of a person's head looking like a hall with a long line of doors. Each one leads into a different part of the person's mind. A childhood would be behind one door, good memories behind another, and all the big bad memories, the ones you wished you could forget, would be locked up tight behind the biggest door of all.

When I walked through the proverbial door that led into the prince's head, I hadn't expected to walk straight into what had to be one of his worst nightmares.

There, standing in the Orchard, was the prince along with Alice. Her face flickered between a tall blonde woman that I could only assume was the princess and what Alice looked like now. Next to them stood the real Princess, Lynne.

The scene looked normal except the princess was wielding a blade in her hand. She had it pointed at the two of them while tears ran down her face. Since this was Lynne and not Kat, plus a dream, I didn't have the overwhelming urge to be near her or to soothe her pain.

"How could you do this to me?" she screamed, waving the dagger at them. "I thought you loved me."

"I do love you, Lynne," the prince argued, reaching for her, but she jerked away from him, the blade just barely missing the palm of his hand.

"If you loved me you wouldn't have been with her. Just admit it, you never loved me at all, did you?" she shouted into his face, "It was just a game arranged by my mother. I'm just a joke to you, in fact, I shouldn't be here at all."

She took the blade she had in her hand and flipped it around so it was pointed toward her heart. The prince cried out and tried to jerk the dagger out of her grasp. At the last moment, instead of trying to stab herself, she twisted it around and shoved it into his stomach with a gleeful grin.

"Lynne, why?" his words came out gurgled as blood dripped from his lips. The prince's hand clutched at the handle protruding from his body. Blood poured from the wound. He fell to his knees as Alice and Lynne conformed into one person.

The prince's eyes widened as a mirror image of himself, sans the knife wound, stared down at him. Someone had a guilty conscious.

The wounded prince collapsed to the ground, a pool of liquid beginning to form around him. The evil version of him stood over his corpse for a moment, laughing at the scene. Then, like something had clicked, the scene started all over again with him kissing Alice and Lynne catching them.

Had this been what he'd been seeing ever since he'd gone to the Shadow Realm? While I was dallying with Morgana and trying to find a way home, he had been suffering alone. His guilt eating him alive.

While the prince was busy replaying his darkest regret, I took a moment to look around. The Orchard was exactly what it looked like in the real world, except with it being in the prince's mind, there seemed to be a dark edging around it. Like the mood of the dream was causing the lights to dim.

Wondering if everything else was like in the real world, I glanced down at myself to see that I was an actual physical person. The clothing I was wearing in the Shadow Realm was the same as what I wore now. Curious about what else could be the same, I reached over and pinched myself. A sharp pain went through my arm, and a red mark appeared where I had marred myself.

So, I could get hurt here. Could I die? Watching the prince stab himself over and over again didn't give me the confidence that I would leave unscathed should I come into contact with the same fate.

I turned my head back and forth wondering if I was stuck in the Orchard or if I could leave? Would I end up in the queen's garden or did it just end? The only way to find out was to move but first...

I took the first step since arriving, my foot crunched in the grass beneath my feet as I wandered over to where the prince was bleeding out. Just as the scene reset itself, and the princess started screeching again, I cleared my throat.

Strangely enough, not just the prince's head turned but all of them did as if they were one body. Seeing as it was the prince's mind, I could imagine they were all him in a way. His mind was filling in the roles of those that tormented him.

"Not that I'm not enjoying you kill yourself over and over again, but we do have a time limit here." I pointed at my wrist, though I wasn't wearing a watch. What I said wasn't exactly true. The Reaper hadn't said I only had such and such amount of time, but I figured the longer I was in here, the more likely I would get stuck. So getting out fast was the best course of action.

In unison, the three heads tilted to the side as they surveyed my form. They seemed confused by my very presence, which didn't bode well for me. I didn't need the prince's brain thinking I was an intruder and have him try to boot me out before I even got started.

"It's me, Cheshire." I started taking a few cautious steps forward. "We both got sent to the Shadow Realm when Kat said the spell."

"Spell?" the word came out of all three of their mouths, but I only heard one voice. The prince's. Good, we were making progress.

"You remember, you decided to join the Shadows and became a certified boarding ship for their magic. Then Kat sent you here, unfortunately, as a side effect of that, I ended up in the Shadow Realm too." I shrugged and sighed. "Nothing seems to go the way we plan it. Oh well."

This time only the prince's form had a reaction. His lips pursed together, and he stepped away from the two women. The moment he cleared them they dissipated. As he walked over to where I stood his expression was still that of confusion. It seemed we weren't as far along as I thought.

"Cheshire?"

"Yep, that's me. Cheshire S. Cat, at your service." I gave a mock bow to him with a cheeky grin.

"What's happened?" he looked around like it was the first time he had truly noticed his surroundings. "Why are we in the Orchard?"

I pointed a finger at him. "That's all on you and your conscious. I had nothing to do with it; I'm just along for the ride."

His eyes darted around as mine had moments ago. Panic filled his face, and I took a small step toward him. He shook his head side to side, his dark hair whipping around him. His hands shook. He gripped his face and started muttering to himself.

"Look, don't have a meltdown now; we have to get out of here." I placed my hands on his shoulders, forcing him to look at me. "I won't be able to get out of your head until we get those Shadows out of here. And as much as I enjoy watching you torture yourself, I'd rather not spend forever with only you as company. Got it?"

He visibly swallowed but nodded, the panic not completely gone from his eyes. "All right." His words came out raspy and tight. "What do we have to do?"

"Well, first," I clapped him on the shoulders before dropping my hands, "we need to figure out where in your mind the Shadows are holding up. Then, we can figure out how to get rid of them."

The prince didn't say anything as I tried to think of where they would go. Could they be back at my Willow Tree? Did it even exist here? Before I could try to think up any other options the prince spoke up.

"I think I know where they are."

"You do?" my eyes lit up with surprise, "well, don't hold back. Where are they?"

He let out a huff as if frustrated with my question. "I do not know exactly where they lie, but I have this feeling," he touched his stomach with his fingertips, "inside of my gut that is pulling at me. And I feel that if we follow it we will find them."

Frowning at his description, but not really having any other ideas, I gestured forward. "Very well, your highness, you lead the way."

"Dorian."

"What?" I cocked my head to the side, not understanding what he was saying to me.

"My name is Dorian. Not prince, not your highness. If you are going to be rummaging through my head you might as well know my real name."

I knew to most Fae giving their real name in this day and age was a big deal. The fact that he entrusted it to me said a lot, especially since he didn't really care for me. Since I didn't have another name but my own, half-breed advantage and all, I played it off as nothing.

"Let's not get all mushy now, get going, there are people waiting for us." I gave him a little shove with my tail as I crossed my arms over my chest.

Dorian started walking toward the entrance to the queen's garden. As I followed behind him, he started to ask questions.

"How long have I been in here?"

"I don't know," I shrugged. "We've been in the Shadow Realm for about six human months now, so I imagine you've probably been asleep this whole time."

"I'm asleep? I don't remember even going to the Shadow Realm, let alone falling asleep." He maneuvered around the green hedges and into the main part of the garden.

I had only come to the queen's garden once in my life. It wasn't really somewhere I cared to be, or somewhere I was welcome, but the time I had come I remembered vaguely wondering about the statue in the middle. Now that I had spoken to the Reaper I knew what that statue signified.

The tree was the seed he had stolen. The two women were the two queens of the Underground and lastly, the man was the Reaper himself. The statue depicted a story that was never told and one that really needed to be.

"I love my mother's garden," the prince, I mean, Dorian commented. His eyes wandered around the area. "I haven't seen it in years. Not since I was exiled. Lynne, I mean, Kat," he caught himself and paused before saying, "she told me to visit my mother since I was now free, but I never did. I was too worried about getting Kat back, thinking I'd have all the time in the world to reunite with my mother. But I didn't know how wrong I was, I didn't even have a chance, did I?"

He looked back at me and I choked. What the hell do you say to the guy who has been trying to steal your girl for the last year? Yeah, sure, she was his first, but she wasn't the same person she was back then. I sure as hell wouldn't have fallen for her if she had been. From what I heard, the princess was about as fun as the queen herself.

"I don't know what kind of chance you had, to be honest," I tried to give him a sympathetic smile, but it came out as more of a grimace, "I just know who she is now, not who she used to be."

He made a humming noise before he held a finger up in thought. "That's what my problem has been. She kept telling me she wasn't Lynne, and I kept thinking she would change back into the woman I loved, but it was foolish of me to try to change her."

"Well, look at it this way," I walked past him toward the entrance to the palace, "you loved her enough to try and get her back. Many would have forgotten their love after so long. Holding on like you did shows loyalty, commitment. One day you'll find someone else that will value those aspects." I gave him a fanged tooth grin. "If not you can always flaunt your Fae crown at them and watch them come running."

Dorian actually laughed at my words, making me feel weird inside. Who was this new prince I was seeing? Where was the broody, cruel, bastard I loved to hate? As I followed him into the palace, I wondered which one was the real him, the one I saw now, or the one he showed the world?

The moment we stepped into the palace I knew we were on the right track. My skin prickled with goose bumps, the sense of evil was thick in the air. Both of our gazes trained to the top of the stairs, where the Shadows had to be.

"Do you feel that?" Dorian asked me, as he moved toward the staircase. "I've never felt something so powerful. So malevolent."

"Yeah," I agreed, my feet slowly moving up behind him. My ears twitched on my head as I tried to keep alert to anything that might jump out at us. My tail wrapped around my leg showing my anxiety in the moment. I didn't want to go up those stairs, but I knew I had to.

Each step made the air thicker and harder to breathe over the power being exuded. We were getting closer to them. That meant soon it would all be over. At least I hoped.

Dorian stopped in front of a door that I didn't recognize. I'd never been to the palace and now was not really the time to be sightseeing. Instead of wondering what it was in the real world, I worried what was behind it here.

When Dorian twisted the handle and swung the door in, my worst fear was realized, and the reason we were here was before us.

The Shadows.

CHAPTER

KAT

I RAN UNTIL my legs gave out on me, and I collapsed in the middle of the fog. I heaved in air until I was on the verge of hyperventilating. Glancing around, I realized I couldn't see a fucking thing. The hand in front of my face was barely visible and it was touching my nose. If that wasn't bad enough, my emotions were running rampant, like a twister inside of me.

What the hell did I just do? Sure, Morgana had been trying to kill me, but I had never lost control to that point. The last time I almost killed someone had been with Tick, but Alice was there to stop me. I thought for sure this time I was going to kill her but then what was up with that tear?

It wasn't like me to get emotional like that. Was my own inner conscience telling me to stop or something else altogether? Either way, the panic inside me from almost committing murder slowly started to dissipate, and then with it, the affects of the fog started seeping in.

A sick feeling settled into the pit of my stomach, and I found it hard to breathe again. The overwhelming urge to just curl up into a ball had me frozen in place.

What the hell was this? I'd been so overwhelmed by my own emotions that I hadn't noticed anything else around me. As I ran into the fog I hadn't thought anything of it. Thoughts whirled through my mind that weren't my own. I didn't belong here. I shouldn't be here.

Paralyzed where I was, I grasped my head with my hands. I rocked back and forth in a soothing motion, but it didn't help. I didn't know long I had been here, or when it would end, but the thought of trying to move at all was terrifying.

Eventually, muffled voices filled the silence, but I could barely hear them over my own dread. I had closed my eyes tight, so I didn't know the figures were approaching me until they are right on me.

"Pathetic," squawked a voice, but I couldn't bring myself to care enough to look up.

"I'll bring her inside," another voice griped.

Something slid underneath me that was soft against the surface of my skin and then I was lifted into the air. Clutching onto whatever I could hold onto, I popped my eyes open to see a brightly colored floral dress beneath my hands.

I'd seen this dress before. My eyes lit up at the realization and then they shot to the face of the person carrying me, or persons I should say.

Type and Gripe, the two-headed sister bird that worked the reception desk in the Between, stared down at me. "Oh, you're awake. We thought we lost you there in the fog."

"Put her down, sister. She can walk," Gripe demanded letting go of my legs suddenly causing them to drop to the ground and me to stumble to my feet. It was then I noticed that the fear I'd been feeling had disappeared. Looking around I realized I was no longer standing in the fog but in a clear pathway that was only around them.

Waving my hands around in confusion, I asked them, "Why aren't you being affected by the fog? It's not even touching you."

"That's because we're supposed to be here, you aren't." Type gave me a know-it-all look as if I was supposed to know that.

"So, then, why are you guys here? Everyone thought you got taken by the Shadows."

"Ha, like they care about us. No, we got exiled by the queen."

"Like it was our fault that the Shadows killed two of her men and busted down the doors," Gripe crossed one arm over their chest and huffed, "like we were supposed to be able to stop it? It's hardly fair."

"I'm happy to see that you're okay," I half-heartedly said as I followed them through the fog, which precariously cleared around us with each step. "How do you know where you're going?"

"You're just outside of our home. We heard you screaming from over there." Type gestured with a wing.

"Your home?"

"Of course, where else do you think we live? Just because we're stuck here doesn't mean that we don't have some amenities," Type continued as we moved out of the fog and into an open area. It looked like the mirror graveyard and the hovel that were in Morgana's area.

Gripe snorted in response to her sister's words, "If you can call them amenities."

"Now, sister, you should be happy we have anything at all. We could be stuck in one of those stupid mirrors. Or worse yet, like the prince."

At the mention of Dorian, my ears perked up. "The prince? Did he come through here? How was he? Was he still..."

"Taken over by the Shadows? Yeah," Gripe squawked, waving her wing in the air, "He breezed through here causing a ruckus and was picked up by the Reaper. They headed back to his place...about...I don't know. How long has it been, sister?"

"Oh, how should I know? I don't even know how long we've been stuck here. I have no clue how long it's been since we saw him." Type glanced at me over her glasses with a pointed look. "It's been awhile, dearie." As if that answered anything at all.

"All right, then, how do I get to the Reaper's?"

At my words the sisters' laughed, putting their hands on their stomach, and throwing their heads back. They laughed quite a bit longer than I thought was necessary for the situation. When they finally stopped, Type said, "Missy, you don't go to the Reaper, he goes to you. Besides, none of us know how to get to where he lives anyways."

"Except that horrible woman, Morgana," Gripe jumped in, making me groan.

Great, the one person I needed help from was the person I had almost popped the eyeballs from her head. I wasn't going back there. So the only thing left for me to do was go forward, but since I couldn't get through the fog without the sisters' there with me, I didn't really have much of a choice but to get the sisters' to be my guide.

"Stop that, we know what you was thinking," Gripe waved a feathered arm in the air, "Don't even look at us. Even if we knew where the Reaper was, we wouldn't take you there. No way, no how. Not on purpose."

"What else am I supposed to do?"

Type gave her sister a look that caused a muttering argument between the two.

"No, I don't want to."

"But she needs help."

"He tried to eat us last time."

"But she could talk to the queen to get us out."

Gripe let out a frustrated growl, throwing her arm up in the air before turning her head away, while Type turned to me.

"There is one other person that could probably help you get to the Reaper's."

"Well, why didn't you say so?" I almost jumped for joy at the prospect of not having to ask Morgana for help. "I thought you said only Morgana knew how to get there."

"Well, that wasn't entirely true. This other person doesn't really like to be disturbed."

Gripe spoke up at that, "Ha! Doesn't like visitors my fanny. If you were a gorgeous High Fae he'd give you the time of day in a minute flat," she snapped her fingers, "But that Cheshire is just as bad as his son. Trying to pollinate all of the flowers."

"Cheshire? You mean Chess' father? I met him through the mirror before I got here. Take me to him, he'll help me, I know it."

"That's where I draw the line. I'm not going anywhere near that mangy cat. No way, no how." Gripe waved her wing in the air, an unrelenting look on her face.

"I can't go into the fog on my own. I need you," I pleaded with the sisters'.

Type looked at her sister and then back to me, her face torn between what to do. Finally, after what felt like forever, a light came on in her eyes.

"Ow!" Gripe yelled as Type pulled a feather from her neck. "What you do that for?"

"Here." Type handed the feather to me and I hesitantly took it into my grasp.

"What's this for?" Unless I was looking to make a feather boa or have some naughty fun, I really didn't see the point of them giving me their feather.

"Try to walk into the fog. Go, go." Type ushered me forward with a flip of her hand.

I cocked an eyebrow but then slowly made my way back to the edge of the fog. Before I could even place one foot inside of it everything inside of me screamed for me to turn back the other way. I had to mentally prep myself to even think about moving into it. Closing my eyes tight, I forced my foot to step into the fog. I waited for that sick feeling to come over me again, but it never came.

My eyes popped open, and I looked around myself, but the fog wasn't there. Just like before when I had been with the sisters', the area around me was clear of the mist, and I could move through it without getting paralyzed.

"Hey, it worked!" I turned back to them and raised my hands up in the air.

Type nodded her head. "Just as I thought. The magic doesn't require the whole person to be in the fog. You just need part of their essence. So hold on to that feather tight and you'll be able to find your way to the cat, who can then help you get to the Reaper's."

Keeping a tight grip on the feather, I nodded my head at the sisters' in thanks and then turned on my heel, heading out into the foggy sea. I'm almost there Chess. Just hold on. I told myself as I trekked forward into the fog.

After a few minutes, I had no idea where I was going. I was completely lost. The sisters' had helped me find a way to get through the fog without it touching me, but they hadn't exactly told me how to get to Cheshire.

Growling in frustration, I gripped my hair and tried to think what to do. I could spend hours out here going in circles and never getting any closer. How could I get a direct line to him? I needed a beacon or guided trail.

That's when I remembered what Cheshire said to me in the mirror. Chess and my connection would help me find the way. Maybe this is what he meant? I just needed to concentrate on my magic and find where he was.

Releasing the breath I was holding, I closed my eyes, dug deep down to my magic and into the hole in my chest where Chess used to be. At first I thought it wasn't working and then suddenly I felt something. A familiar twinge that set my eyes shooting up and my feet moving forward.

I knew exactly where he was; I didn't need to go to his dad at all. I kept moving forward, my feet leading the way until the ground beneath my feet turned into stone and the fog around me dissipated. A large

Coliseum like building that reminded me of those monuments they had in Greece, stood before me. It only made sense that it was the Reaper's home. Since he was pretty much the lord of the dead it was only fitting that he'd have a palace.

My feet made no sound as I made my way across the stone path surrounded by water. I tried to keep my eye on the prize, and by that, I meant Chess' hunky form, but a light caught my attention, drawing my gaze from the entrance to the Greek palace to the water along the path. Swirling blue objects swam in the water. My lips ticked up as I realized they looked like some kind of magical sperm.

For magical jizz they sure were hypnotizing, I thought as I leaned down toward them. My hand reached out on its own, and as my fingers brushed the surface, the weird little swirls latched onto me. They pulled the feet out from under me jerking me from the path and into the freezing water.

Holding my breath, my eyes widened as the glowing things became more like leeches that were trying to drown me. They latched onto any skin they could find and began to pulsate around me. I could feel my magic being drained from me as more and more of them found their way to me.

I tried to claw at them, but my fingers just slipped through their bodies. My heart pounded in my chest as I began to really panic. Though, I couldn't touch them, the weight of their bodies made it close to impossible to move, let alone swim to the surface. I fought to move my arms and legs, but my energy was completely zapped, and I was running out of breath. I'd never been a great swimmer, preferring to lounge than to actually exercise. At this point, my lungs were burning from the extended length I had been underwater, and I thought for sure I was going to die.

Then, by some miracle, the little bugger suddenly ripped away from me. If they'd had mouths I was sure they would have been squealing in fright as they scurried away. My body became lighter, and I struggled to move toward the surface. My eyes were only half open, my will to live and oxygen low, so I couldn't make out the blurry figure that cast a shadow over where I floated in the water.

Hands reached down and grabbed me beneath my arms. They pulled me through the water and as I broke the surface, I let out a gasp. That gasp turned into a coughing fit as the water that had managed to find its way into my lungs decided it changed its mind and wanted out of this joint; I didn't blame it. I was beginning to wish I had never come.

Taking in the air like it was going out of fashion, I lay on the stone ground, my savior having the opportunity to decide if they wanted to finish the job the little shits had started or not.

My eyes fluttered open and made contact with a black cloak with no feet. Frowning, I forced myself to become more aware as my eyes trailed up the long cloak and over the broad chest to land on a face so familiar to me. The dark blue eyes on the handsome face shot through me and to the place where I held the little pieces of my previous self.

Dorian. Wait, no. It wasn't Dorian. He looked kind of like him but not exactly. Maybe a relative? Whoever he was, he'd saved me, and I wasn't about to look a gift horse in the mouth.

"You must be Chess' lady friend that's come to save him." He held a hand out to me, which I readily accepted.

"That would be me." I coughed as I came to my feet. "Savior and all that, but you can call me Kat."

"Very well, Kat," he said, his lips twitching at the edges. I knew what he was thinking. My name was Kat and I'm dating a Fae cat. Ironic I know. It wasn't like I hadn't thought of that myself but bringing it up just didn't seem important. Maybe I would just start going by Moderator so people would stop being surprised by it.

"Your feline friend, I am afraid is otherwise occupied, but you are free to wait for him to finish his task." The man who I could only assume was the Reaper moved past me and toward the large doors of the building. Opening up the door, he gestured inside, "Please come into my home."

Raising a wary brow at him, I questioned, "How do I know you aren't just going to hold me prisoner like you are doing Chess? I'm supposed to be saving him from you, not becoming buddies."

The Reaper laughed, he threw his head back, making his dark hair cascade down his back. "I can see why the feline is so taken with you as well as my son."

"Your son?" That had me moving. I had been right, he was related to Dorian. But I would never in all my years have guessed that he was his father. Dorian's dad was the Reaper, who'd have figured. Actually, take that back. With as creepy as his mother was and brooding as Dorian could be, I could totally see those two getting together and making a Fae prince baby.

Not answering my question, he entered the building assuming I would follow. I didn't disappoint and hurried in after him.

Inside, was no different than what I expected a Greek palace to look like. Large columns and high ceilings, it would put my mother's palace to shame.

I didn't pay much attention to the decor as we came upon the top of the room where a large slab of rock sat. On that rock lay Dorian's body wrapped in blue energy and standing next to him was...

"Chess!" I ran across the room and stood by his side. When he didn't turn immediately at my call I knew something was up. Placing a hand on his shoulder, I dipped around to look at his face.

His eyes were closed and his face scrunched down in concentration. One hand was lying on Dorian's chest, and the magic surrounding Dorian's body was wrapped around his hand. Dorian's veins were filled with black and pulsated under his skin.

"What's wrong with them?" I asked the Reaper as he came up beside me. I didn't drop my hand from Chess' shoulder, just the contact with him made me feel better. I could feel the hole in my heart start to close, and my body felt lighter as if a huge weight had lifted.

"The Shadows are still in my son and your beau is helping me to get them out. Once he has then he will be free to leave this place."

I frowned hard at the Reaper's explanation. "But what if he can't get them out?"

He shook his head, a deep sadness in his expression. "Then they will be both stuck in his mind forever, to forcefully remove him would kill not just my son but possibly him as well. Then it would have been all for naught."

I looked back to Chess and Dorian, a fist clenched around my heart. I had just found them again and now I was at risk of losing them both. I couldn't let it happen. I wouldn't.

I turned to the Reaper with determination on my face. "What can I do?"

He gave me a grim smile. "Exactly what you are. Give him your support. Just being at his side will make him more powerful, and hopefully that will be enough to get them both out alive."

Hopefully? I didn't like the sound of that, not one bit.

CHAPTER

CHESS

THE ROOM LOOKED as if once upon a time it could have been someone's bedroom. Now, though, it was covered in darkness, the furniture in the room barely visible through the billowing energy coming from one side of the room. Just standing in the doorway made my skin crawl.

"So, what's the plan?" I peeked over at Dorian, who stood by my side, his rigid frame telling me he was feeling exactly what I was feeling if not more so. He'd had this thing inside of him for so long it probably affected him worse than me.

"Plan?" he gave me a quick look before his eyes trained back on the slithering form before us. "What plan? You are supposed to save me, remember? What do you think we should do?"

I was hoping he wouldn't say that. Sure, I had jumped in feet first knowing that the likelihood of me coming out was slim, but I hadn't thought of what to do once we got in here. How the heck were we supposed to expel that massive thing from his body?

My eyes searched the room, my brain scrambling for some sort of idea. I don't know what happened but the next thing I knew I was thrown off balance, a sharp pain in my heart. Kneeling on the ground, I clutched my hand to my chest and hissed.

"Cheshire?" the prince looked down on me. "Are you all right? What was that?"

I shook my head. "I don't know. There was this pain right here." I patted my chest and winced.

"Could your body be being tampered with?"

"I don't think so, the Reaper was standing guard. I doubt anyone would try to mess with us with him there." I thought for a moment, accessing the pain in my chest, and then realized what it was. The hole. The hole was closing up. It had been open so long that the force of it closing had brought me physical pain, and if it was closing that could only mean one thing.

"Kat!" I cried out, jumping to my feet. "She's here. She's beside us. I can...I can feel her." I placed a hand on my shoulder where a weight had appeared.

"Good, then she can watch us both die if we don't figure out what to do about this," he said bitterly waving a hand in front of him, "Why not ask her if she has any ideas?"

I gave him a pointed look. "It doesn't work that way. We are connected, yes, but I'm not in my mind right now, it wouldn't be possible to contact her. But now that she is here, my magic is complete again." A slow smirk climbed up my face, and I stretched my arms over my head, a renewed strength plowing through me, filling my veins with power. "And that means these guys don't have a chance."

"Powerful or not, we are not going to get far if we do not have a plan," the prince pointed out with a raised brow.

Unfortunately, he was right. Fattened with power, I was being cocky, and that could get me killed if I approached this the wrong way. My eyes scanned the room once more. They landed on the corner of the room where the darkness was the thickest.

Squinting my eyes, I could barely make out an object on the wall. It was a mirror! That must be where they were latching on to Dorian.

"Do you see that over there?" I tried to discreetly point to the corner of the room. "Do you think if we destroy it then they wouldn't be able to hold on to you anymore?"

Before the prince could answer me, the malevolent energy in the room started to coil and churn. Screaming voices came from the cloud. They were too jumbled up to make out clearly. The wind from their screams blew at us forcing us back from the doorway and into the hall. The moment we were in the clear, the door slammed shut in front of us.

"I guess that answers that question." I dusted myself off as I picked myself up off the floor. Dorian climbed to his feet as well, standing beside me with intensity in his eyes that I hoped would never be directed at me.

"They are just playing with us," he snarled at the door, "they knew we were here the whole time and were just laughing as we quivered in our boots. Now, though," he pushed his sleeves back with a nasty grin, "We know how to defeat them."

"Yeah, but they shoved us out. How are we going to get to the mirror to destroy it?" I stared hard at the door envisioning where the mirror was on the other side. There had to be some way to get to it without getting blasted back out again.

"You leave that to me," Dorian said with a confidence I didn't have. "I will be the diversion while you get to the mirror."

"Right." I pumped my fists and then gave him a curious look. "What exactly are you going to do?"

"Something very prince-like." His lips broadened into an all-out grin and then he started for the door. Ignoring the handle, Dorian lifted a foot and kicked the door. It went flying across the room and smashed on the opposite wall.

"Whoa!" I exclaimed at his strength. "If you could do that why didn't you do it before?"

He shrugged and said, "I just now realized we are inside my head, so that means I can do whatever I want. Thus, kicking down the door." He gestured to where it lay in pieces on the floor. "Let's see them keep us out now."

We stepped back into the room, and the Shadows went berserk. They tried to blow us out again, but we were ready for them this time. Holding our ground, we forced our way in, the shrieking of the lost souls ringing in our ears.

"It's all you, princey." I gestured forward.

Dorian frowned at me, probably not liking my nickname for him, before he took a step forward, he held up a finger. "Excuse me."

The Shadows stopped whipping around the room, their screeches becoming a dull roar. It was interesting that just his voice would command such attention. Probably had something to do with him being the Reaper's son.

Shrugging at the thought, I watched as he came right up to where the Shadows had conformed together near the bed. The form they made was almost that of a man but without a mouth or eyes to see out of. Dorian didn't seem to let this bother him, because he started talking to it.

"Are you aware that you are trespassing in my head?"

The Shadows laughed, the sound of it ground on my nerves and burned my ears. "We were invited, you cannot send us away now."

"Apparently, you do not know when you are not wanted." He shook a finger at the figure, the absurdity of the act making me smile. "Now, I command you to leave my head at once." The haughtiness in his tone left no room for argument, if only the Shadows felt that way.

The Shadows did not take kindly to being commanded, and they reached out for the prince. While the Shadows were busy with Dorian, I made my way over to the mirror. When I stepped into the darkness chills covered my skin, and I had to force myself to walk forward even though everything in me was screaming to turn back.

Just short of crawling, I finally made it to the mirror. Staring into it was a bit strange. The reflection looking back at me wasn't myself. It looked like me but was more of a shadow replica. My eyes glowed and a dark aura surrounded my body, I had to look down at myself to make sure it was actually in the mirror and not what was really happening. Thankfully, it was just my reflection that looked that way. The Shadows were trying to throw me off.

I glanced around for something to break the glass with and found a statue of the queen's head lying on the floor. Reaching down slowly, as to not spook the man in the reflection, I wasn't surprised to see that he did not move with me. I picked the statue up, its heavy weight filling my hands.

Before I could smash it against the glass, though, the man in the mirror spoke, "You do not want to do that, Cheshire." His voice sounded like mine but with an echoing affect that dashed any illusion of him being me.

"Oh, I assure, I do." I held the statue up ready to slam it against the glass but was once more stopped by the voice.

"They are lying to you," the voice of my shadow self said, "they wish you to destroy us because they know we are right. We are Fae and should walk the human world as gods, not cower in fear to their rules and armies."

My arms let the statue drop slightly, and I leaned toward the mirror as I said, "It is that kind of attitude that had me beaten and parentless before I reached puberty. That high and mighty thinking will only get you killed. I won't let what was done to me be done to anyone else."

"But we could help you," he implored, "We could make you a king. Then all those who cast you aside would bow down at your feet. Can't you just imagine it?"

I actually could. When I was younger I had dreamed that very same dream over and over again, hoping one day for it to come true. That was back before I met Kat. Now, I realized that the only way I was going to get what I wanted, and have people look at me the way I wanted them to, was to make it happen myself. I couldn't control what they thought about me, but I could control how I reacted to them. I wasn't going to be any body's puppet, not anymore.

"Hurry up already, would you?" Dorian's voice cut into my thoughts, and I chanced a glance over to where he was beating off the shadows that were trying to grab him. Looks like the gig was up.

"You can't help me," I said to my reflection, "Only I can help myself, and you? You're done." I smashed the statue against the mirror, and at first, nothing happened. Then a crack started where I had hit it. Just a tiny one, and then that small crack splintered out into more, until the entire mirror was covered with them.

Before he became completely erased the shadow image of myself smiled. "You will regret this, cat. We will make you wish you had taken our bargain."

"Not in this lifetime." As the words fell from my mouth there was an explosion that threw me across the room. The glass shattered, and the piercing screams were back. I clutched my head but it didn't help. They were inside my mind, and I couldn't make them stop. Before long it was too much for me to handle, and everything went black.

The darkness didn't last long, because I was shoved quite forcefully back into my body. My eyes snapped open and I found myself staring up at the face of the one person I had been craving to see. Kat.

"Hey, you. It's nice to have you back." She smiled down at me and then her face changed. She frowned hard, and her eyes glinted with anger. Grabbing me by the shoulders, she shook me with all her might. "Don't you ever do anything like that again! Do you hear me? I thought I lost you!"

She threw me down to the ground and then pulled me up again and into her arms. My eyes wobbled in my head from her treatment. I could only let her hug me. Then when my brain finally settled, I wrapped my arms around her, tucking my face into her neck, just to breathe her in. She smelled like home, and I was never leaving her again.

CHAPTER

KAT

I COULDN'T BELIEVE I finally had him back. It felt like forever since I had been in his arms, and now that I was finally here, I couldn't imagine ever letting go.

Chess didn't seem to have any inclination to release me either, and we would have probably stayed like that forever, just holding each other had a throat not cleared near us.

"While, this is all very touching," the Reaper's voice cut into the air, causing Chess and I to pull back from each other but not let go. "We have a bigger problem at hand."

"What's that?" I asked from my spot on the floor where Chess had collapsed.

"While we were able to dispel the Shadows from my body we weren't able to destroy them completely." Dorian stepped over to us. The blue energy no longer covered him and his veins had gone back to normal. I had to say I was relieved to see him like his old self again. I couldn't deal with an evil Dorian much longer.

"Then where did they go?" Chess asked as he climbed to his feet. He held a hand out to me, which I took and let myself be drawn to my feet.

"Right before you two woke up, the darkness in your veins," he directed toward Dorian, "came together to center at your heart. Then all at once it burst out of you and shot into the sky." The way he described it was exactly what had happened. I was paying too much attention to making sure Chess was all right to really get all the gory details, but I had seen the darkness shoot out of Dorian. At that same time though, Chess had collapsed to the ground, so where they went afterward I didn't know.

"They didn't stay here long, probably thought it was best to regroup before trying to attack again. It takes a lot of energy to take a living hosts body and then to be ejected the way they were," the Reaper paused and shook his head, "they are probably licking their wounds out there somewhere." The Reaper shrugged and then pointed toward the entrance. Our eyes followed his finger to where the door was wide open but no Shadows were in sight.

"All right then." I clapped my hands and rubbed them together. "Looks like it's time to hunt down some Shadows." I grabbed Chess' hand in mine with a smile that he returned and started toward the door, but I was stopped by the Reaper's hand on my shoulder.

"No," he stated, making me frown.

"No? What do you mean no? They got out, they're not dead yet so that means they can still come back again." I felt the anger billow up in me at the prospect of having to fight them off once more so they didn't kill my friends and family. "We can't give them a chance to get strong again, or we might never destroy them, and next time they might get out into the human world."

"You are correct." The Reaper nodded, but he held his hand up before I could interject as to why the fuck he was holding me back. "But this is not your world. You don't belong here, and if you go searching for the Shadows, you will find more danger for yourself than just the enemy you seek."

A bit of fear filled me at his words. I'd already had to make it through the fog that didn't want me here and the glowing leeches that tried to drown me. Who knew what other baddies waited for me out there?

"Then who's going to go after them, then?" I gestured violently to the door. "It's partly my fault they are wreaking havoc on the world. I should be the one to stop them. I did it before."

The Reaper huffed. "And look where that got you. The spell you were given was a temporary fix. It was only meant to get them back here, not to destroy them."

It wasn't? Before I could voice my question, Chess stepped in, "Then why did the Seelie Queen give Kat that spell to begin with?" Chess snarled.

"Things are a bit more complicated then all that, my dear Cheshire," the Reaper said, guilt spreading across his face briefly before it disappeared, but I had seen it and knew why.

"The Seelie Queen knew who really let the Shadows out, didn't she?" the look I gave the Reaper was accusatory, daring him to lie to my face. I knew the answer to the question. The culprit had told me who the guilty party was already. "You gave her the spell to get them back here so you could clean up yours and Mab's mess. Am I wrong?"

The Reaper did not say anything for a moment and then looked to Dorian. I could tell that he wanted to tell him he was his father; I could see it on the tip of his lips. But saying so would also mean admitting that the reason that the Shadows got out was because he and Mab had been seeing each other via the mirror in her bedroom, giving the Shadows the perfect escape route.

"Tell him," Chess interrupted my thoughts prodding the Reaper. "Tell him what he needs to know. It won't be any easier later."

Still the Reaper hesitated, but it didn't matter because Dorian spoke up, "I know already."

249

"You do?" his father's eyebrows lifted at his words.

Dorian gave a bitter laugh and rubbed the back of his neck. "I might have been cursed and more recently overtaken by the Shadows, but that has not affected my ability to see what is right in front of my face," he paused for a moment putting us all on the edge of our seat, "you're my father."

"How...did your mother...?" the Reaper stumbled over his words as Dorian gave him a lopsided grin, one I hadn't seen in years.

"No, you can feel safe in knowing she never betrayed your trust. I was quite in the dark until I woke up just a few moments ago." He gave his father a small smile, and shrugged his shoulders. "Seeing you was like looking in a mirror. I just knew."

The Reaper nodded as if he knew exactly what Dorian was talking about. I was glad one of them did, because I sure as hell didn't. If I had woke up after fighting for my life, the first thing on my mind wouldn't be 'Oh, that guy's my dad.' No, it would be more like where is the fucking tequila?

Guess that was one reason Dorian and I would never be good for each other. Which would be a problem if I was not already so over the heels in love with the Fae next to me that looked just as confused as I was.

"Good. Great. Congratulations," I interrupted them before they started getting all mushy and hugging. "Can we get back to the matter at hand? The Shadows are loose. I can't go after them. What are we going to do?"

The Reaper looked to me, his face a bit startled by my abruptness. What could I say? I was a people pleaser.

"I apologize." He bowed his head slightly to me. "I got caught up in the moment. Where were we?"

"You were about to tell everyone that the reason the Shadows got out in the first place was because you and D's mom here fucked up because you couldn't keep the secret portal you were using to see each other on the down low."

Everyone's eyes, and by everyone, I meant Chess and Dorian's, turned to the Reaper, whose face was turning a molting shade of purple. I clamped my mouth shut realizing I probably shouldn't be provoking

251

the guy who would be taking my dead ass to the afterlife. Apparently, almost losing the love of my life again had a negative effect on my need to placate the guy in charge.

"Yes, as you so elegantly put it," he shot me a nasty glare before looking to his son, "the Shadows were able to leave the Shadow Realm because of your mother and mine's door way that we kept open so that we may visit each other." He ran a hand through his hair, a very Dorian like gesture and sighed. "I might be stuck here for the term of my life, but I will be damned if I have to spend it alone."

"I understand," Dorian graciously replied, his answer way more eloquent than mine would have been.

"And because it is my fault," his eyes locked onto me as if daring me to say anything else, but I wasn't biting. My lips were shut tighter than a church girl's on Sunday. I gave him a small smile causing him to continue, "It is only fair that I be the one that takes them down the rest of the way."

"Great." I clapped my hands together and then searched left and right. "Now that that is settled, how do we blow this joint?"

"Blow this joint?" Dorian glanced at me and then to his father, confusion etched on his face.

"It is a human phrase," the Reaper explained, "one of many that I myself have never understood." He shook his head and then crossed his arms. "As for getting out of here, you will not be able to go back the way you came."

"Good," I jumped in. "I didn't particularly want to go through that mess again, and Morgana is not exactly my biggest fan."

"Morgana?" Dorian asked.

"She fancies herself the Queen of the Shadow Realm," Chess said with a grin.

"She doesn't fancy herself anything. She is the Queen of the Shadow Realm," the Reaper said making Chess' face fall.

"But why does she live out there and you live here?" Chess gestured toward the large area.

The Reaper's gaze hardened at the question. "That is a story better left for another time. Now," he twisted around and stared into a darkened area, "if you are done with your questions, the Shadows are getting further away the longer we stand here talking."

"Right." We followed the Reaper until he stopped at a wall. A torch near us lit with a blue flame at our approach.

An metal clinking sounded as the Reaper pulled something out of his pocket. It was a ring of keys. He flipped through them until he stopped on the right one. He held the key out and started to put it into the door.

"Wait."

The sound of Dorian's voice caused us to pause and spin around to look at him. "I am not coming with you."

"You're not?" I glanced at Chess and then at the Reaper before back to Dorian. "Where else are you going to go? You can't stay here, and your mother is waiting for you."

Shaking his head, he trained his eyes on his father's form. "I can still feel them." He placed a hand on his chest, and looked down. "Even though they are no longer inside of me it's like we are still connected. I can feel their anger and their pain." His eyes turned up, sadness and determination there. "They are hurt but their rage is greater. They won't stay placated for long. I can help you find them."

"But wait, you can't..." I started, but Chess placed a hand on my arm. "You can't seriously think that it's a good idea, can you?"

Chess didn't answer me for a moment as he exchanged a look with the Reaper. It seemed I was missing something, but knowing Chess he would tell me eventually. When he did speak he spoke directly to Dorian.

"I think you should spend some time with your father and chasing the Shadows would be a good opportunity to get to know him and the world he lives in."

"Thank you for understanding." Dorian held a hand out to Chess who clasped his hand in his. The look they were exchanging was of mutual respect and some kind of broship that I could never be a part of. What happened while he was in Dorian's head?

"If you are sure?" the Reaper asked Dorian, an uncertainty in his voice, "then I would glad to have you. They are even harder to deal with in their spirit form; I could use all the help I can get."

Frowning, I took a step toward Dorian. "I don't know what to say," I gave him a weak smile, "I'm sorry that we didn't end up the way you wanted us to be."

He gave me a sad smile. "Our time ended a long time ago, you are a different person now, and you ended up with the best man for you." His eyes flicked to Chess, who puffed his chest out and wrapped an arm around my shoulders.

"I guess," I drew out, not exactly sure what was going on. What happened to the arrogant asshole that I'd been dealing with? This new Dorian was freaking me out. Then I met Chess' eyes, and he nodded at me. "Yeah, I guess I did."

"Do not worry," Dorian continued, "this is not goodbye. I still have to find my own happy ending. I am just taking a detour for a little while. Be sure to tell my mother?"

"Of course." I nodded and then suddenly, without provocation I threw myself at him. Hugging him tight around the waist. Tears slid down my face. "I don't know why I'm crying," I said wiping the wetness from my cheeks, and I drew myself away from the now stiff prince.

"It is understandable." Dorian placed his hands on my shoulder. "You might be Kat, but you still have part of Lynne in you. It is she that sheds tears for me, and that means more to me than you can ever know."

I blinked up at him and realized he was right. While I was me; I was also Lynne. I couldn't just ignore my past because it was a part of me and where I am today.

Chess placed a hand on my shoulder, and I turned my gaze to him wondering how he felt about my little outburst. "Are you ready to go home?"

My lips curled up. "Yes, let's go home."

CHAPTER

CHESS

THE REAPER TWISTED the key in the door lock and turned the knob. Throwing the door open, he gestured for us to head inside.

After being in the dark area for so long, the bright white light coming from the doorway hurt my eyes. Squinting into the opening, my mouth dropped open, and then Kat said the exact words I was thinking.

"You have a door to the Between?"

Eugene gave her such a condescending smile that I wanted to jump in and say exactly what he wasn't telling Dorian about staying there. But thankfully, I thought better of it and kept my lips zipped.

"You didn't think I was the Reaper for only the Fae, did you? It would take too long to go all the way through the Underground just to gather souls in your world."

"No, I suppose not," she drew out. Something lit up in her eyes, and she pointed a finger at him. "Wait a second. The first time I came to the Between I swore I saw a dark figure out in the middle of it all. Was that you?"

His lips turned up in to a smirk. "I had to see what all the fuss was about. It was the first time a human came into the Between in over a hundred years, I was sure that meant things would be changing soon. And you know what?" he gestured around us with a wide knowing grin, "I was right."

Chuckling, I grabbed Kat's hand in mine. "You sure were, and I'm thankful every day that she found her way into our world. I don't know what I'd have done without her." The blush that blossomed on her face warmed my heart and even more so when her own emotions became so big that they leaked over into me.

All the love she felt for me engulfed me like a glove, and I had the overwhelming urge to kiss her right then and there. But the way that Dorian and his father were already looking at us said they were getting impatient to get going. So, instead, I led Kat by the hand and toward the door.

"Thank you for everything." I nodded at the Reaper and then looked to Dorian. "And good luck. I hope to see you again."

"We both do," Kat added in, wrapping her arm around me and squeezing me tight. "Now let's get out of here, we have some lost time to make up for." Before I could say another word she dragged me out of the Reaper's home and into the Between.

As we stepped into the Between, the Reaper called out to us, "Just keep going forward, the reception will appear in front of you in no time and above all else, don't get distracted."

An unsettling feeling filled me at his words, but Kat dragged me by the hand, not letting me linger on them.

My eyes stayed on the back of Kat's head. She followed the Reaper's directions to the letter. After a few minutes, the sight of the reception area in the distance broke up the white blankness around us. Kat and I increased our speed, both of us in a hurry to get home and out of this place.

Before we made it to the reception area though, Kat stopped abruptly. She angled her head toward the side and murmured, "Do you hear that?"

I shook my head. I didn't hear anything. I opened my mouth to tell her as much, but she let go of my hand and took a step to the left, off the path and away from where our exit was at.

"I swear, I hear a child crying." She circled around me before stopping back in front of me, her eyes filled with concern. "Are you sure you don't hear anything?"

"No, I'm sorry, love, I don't hear anything at all. It's quiet." I eyed the door to the human world that was just out of our reach and then glanced back at her. "Too quiet for my liking. Let's just get home then we can worry about it later." I placed my hand on her arm, trying to steer her toward our way out, but she jerked away.

"No. I can't just leave them." Her eyes widened and the panic on her face slipped into me. "What if it's lost or hurt? We don't know what is out there." She shook her head profusely. "No. We have to find it."

Kat darted toward where I could only assume she heard the child's cry. I didn't hear anything, and I was beginning to think it was part of what the Reaper had warned us about. Not to leave the path for any reason. That's exactly what Kat was doing. I just got her back. I wasn't losing her again. Not ever, even if she hated me for it later.

Keeping my eye on the reception area, I let my long legs carry me until I caught up to Kat. I grabbed her by the waist and spun her around. "Kat, pet, we are leaving. It's a trick to get you off the path and it's working."

"No, it's not a trick," she yelled at me and tried to twist out of my grasp, "I can hear them, I can."

"No," I grabbed both of her arms and looked her dead in the eye, "you can't. My hearing is ten times better than yours, and if I can't hear it that means it's not really there."

She looked at me for a moment, her face contemplating what I was saying. I almost thought I had gotten through to her but her head angled just slightly enough to give me a warning before she tried to get away from me again. This time though, I picked her up and threw her over my shoulder.

"Put me down!" Kat screamed at me as she beat me with her arms and legs. "I have to get to them. You are killing them by stopping me."

It broke my heart to have to do this to her, but there was no other way. We didn't know what was out there, it could be a child, or for all I knew it could be something that ate children. What I did know was neither of us knew enough about the Between to just run out into it without a care. We'd been through enough; let someone else save the day.

I endured Kat's assault on my person until we got to the reception area where her fighting promptly stopped. The panic in her that I had felt before had dissipated and all that was left was a calm confusion.

"You can let me down now. I'm fine."

I hesitated for a moment before slowly lowering her to the ground. "Are you all right?" I brushed a stray piece of hair behind her ear with a frown.

"Yes," she breathed out and then looked out into the void. "The crying stopped, I don't hear anything now. I don't know why I freaked out like that."

"It's the Between," I assured her, holding her in my arms in case she decided to bolt again. "The Reaper said it would try to trick us. To make us leave the path."

"It's a good thing you were here then," Kat gave me a small smile and then frowned, "I wonder what is out there."

"Not anything good, I can assure you." I walked us over to the door to the human world and twisted the handle. Opening the door, I gestured her inside with a lopsided grin, "besides, don't you have enough on your plate, Miss Moderator?"

"Don't call me that." she scowled at me and punched me on the arm before dragging me inside the portal with her. Finally we were on our way home.

EPILOGUE

KAT

THERE WAS ONE thing I could say about my life now. It's never boring. Not only was I a Seelie Princess, but I was also the moderator for the Fae dwelling in the human world.

What I thought would be an easy job quickly turned into one instance after another. After the initial shock of the Shadows had faded, some of the Fae had gotten it into their heads that it would be okay to do whatever the hell they pleased.

After a few months of jumping from state to state via the mirror portals, I eventually turned to the council in the Underground for help. Together with them, we created another council that would help moderate the Fae on the human side. Now, I was no longer judge and jury but sort of like a bounty hunter. Except without the leather jacket and mullet.

After that, life became a bit easier, and I almost started to have a sense of normalcy. Sometimes I did get called in on random cases by the government. They had since made nice after a visit from the queens' and the council. Seems like my mother knew how to charm the Underground but also presidents as well.

I enjoyed getting called by them on jobs. They were always something fun and exciting. Not like the times my mother asked me for help, which usually involved something painful. Also, they actually paid me. Thank God for my human parent's income, or I'd be out on the streets.

I had been right about Alice. She was a natural born leader. The moment she stepped in to take over as the representative of the Fae community, the easier everything became. I still had to step in every once in a while to knock some sense into those who got out of line, but for the most part, I left everything to her.

Thankfully, Alice eventually moved out of my grandmother's house and into a place of her own in town. Hatter and she were shacking up, not that it was a surprise to anyone. They publicly dated now, but anytime they hold hands or show any kind affection in public, Alice flares up like a firework. It's pretty hilarious since Hatter seems to do it more and more just to get a reaction out of her.

My own love life? It's not too shabby if I do say so myself. Which I do. While I'm the moderator on the human side, Chess took up his position once more as moderator in the Underground. When we both aren't hunting down mischievous Fae we spend our time at his willow tree or at my grandmother's house.

I hadn't heard from Dorian, but I had heard from his mother. She said he was off with his father, still trying to hunt down the Shadows. They were slippery buggers that was for sure. I didn't envy him one bit. I just hoped they kept them in the Shadow Realm this time; I needed a bit of peace and quiet in my life. Not that my human mother didn't keep me hopping with the rest of them.

The best day of my life was the look on her face when Chess showed her his true form for the first time. Her eyes got as wide as saucers; she looked him over, and then pointed at him while looking at me. "Is he...a cat?"

I had gleefully nodded and then almost jumped for joy when she promptly passed out on her Persian rug. My mother was still cautious around Chess to this day. Which was fine with me, because that meant less time for her to pester me into doing talk shows and the like. It was the little things in life that kept things interesting, really.

My grandmother finally came home from Florida. It took her long enough. I swore she had died and no one thought to tell us. Or maybe they just couldn't find the body.

The moment my grandmother had stepped through the door she wrapped me in a hug and then waved a finger in my face. "I had to find out on my own that my granddaughter was a faerie princess through the television. Why didn't you call me?"

Anyways, she had heard about the Fae incidents on the news and someone had leaked a picture of me that they were broadcasting all over the world. Of course, it was the most atrocious picture they could find. It was one from my senior year at high school, when I'd been going through my Goth phase. So, of course that meant I was in all black and had a scary look on my face. God only knew what the world thought of the heathen that kept the Fae in line. Or, well, tried to.

After apologizing profusely for letting her get blindsided, she wanted to know all the hairy details. How it started. Who the lovely gentleman gracing her living room was? She didn't even try to hide the way her eyes greedily took him in.

I chuckled and exchanged a look with Chess who was already well on his way to charming the pants off of her, and I said, "Well, it's a long story. You see, it all started one night with this damn rabbit."

About the Author

Erin Bedford is an otaku, recovering coffee addict, and Legend of Zelda fanatic. Her brain is so full of stories that need to be told that she must get them out or explode into a million screaming chibis. Obsessed with fairy tales and bad boys, she hasn't found a story she can't twist to match her deviant mind full of innuendos, snarky humor, and dream guys.

On the outside, she's a work from home mom and bookbinger. One the inside, she's a thirteen-year-old boy screaming to get out and tell you the pervy joke they found online. As an ex-computer programmer, she dreams of one day combining her love for writing and college credits to make the ultimate video game!

Until then, when she's not writing, Erin is devouring as many books as possible on her quest to have the biggest book gut of all time. She's written over thirty books, ranging from paranormal romance, urban fantasy, and even scifi romance.

Come chat me up

Made in the USA
Monee, IL
15 July 2022

99757351R00154